I0535442

In The Shadows of the Cavern of Death

(Shadows of Death, #1)

by

Angelique Jones

This book is a work of fiction.

Table of Contents

Chapter 1

The darkness surrounded me. The cold seeped into my bones, hidden deep within the ground, where not even a hint of the sun's rays could penetrate. This is where we were forced to make our homes after the cleansing. To many, death is a friend, a way to escape the destruction of the world above. At least we assume that it still remains so above us; so many years have passed that none really know what lies above any longer. The great cleansing destroyed all. War had been inevitable; the population had become a parasite, taking from those who worked until there was nothing left to give. It was not a war between races or of the rich against the poor, but a war of the Contributors against the takers. The government sided with the takers, itself no different than the takers themselves, who far outnumbered the Contributors. Thinking that we would be easily crushed, they were not prepared for what had begun. Brother fought against brother. A civil war raged for years on end. Streets ran red with blood. Bombs fell from the sky like black rain, triggering the natural disasters that finished the world above, destroying all life.

In a last chance to save those who remained, we retreated deep into the ground and built cities into the hardened rocks. In a bid to save what was left of the population, treaties were made and the government resumed control and we became slaves to its whims once more. Supplies were scarce and sacrifices had to be made. Again we were the ones to make them. In a bid to control the population, a lottery was formed: each year during their twenty-first year of life, all must make a journey. Out of the thousands who make this journey, only one hundred will live to see the next day. It is a form of population control to ensure that overcrowding does not occur, but it is more than that, as with age comes wisdom. A wisdom to see the truth of our society that they wish for none to ever see again. All females are required to breed from their seventeenth to twentieth year to ensure workers for the system. Their children are left to the younger members of their families to raise, who are children themselves. If for some reason there are no younger members, the children are turned over to the state and trained as lap dogs of the government. Military soldiers kept separate from the rest of us. Hidden behind masks and armor as cold and unfeeling as the stone that surrounds us.

High above the city, I looked down; it stretched for miles upon miles, too far for the eye to see. The light from the fires that litter the street gave a sinister glow to the run-down houses that we called home. Electricity is a privilege to those like us. A thing we have not earned this month. Everything must be earned, from the very breath that you take, to the bites of food you hoard to fill your crying child's empty stomach. To live in this world you must fight. Nothing is for free, which is not the problem. The problem is no matter how hard you work, it won't matter. For people like me, you are born, you work, you die, and there is nothing more. Our government is run by our current benevolent President Vellion, who the few Elders we have among us that have reached the ripe age of their forties say is the worst they have ever seen. He rules us with an iron fist. When women had stopped breeding, not wanting to leave their children behind as they were left, he had hundreds of women ripped from their homes and taken away. Within a month they were returned. Thrown from trucks by laughing soldiers, beaten, bloody, pregnant, and fearful of a man's touch as a warning to all others. When weeping caregivers carried their starving children through the street begging for mercy, they were taken away never to be heard from again.

Not all places are like this. There are other cities where the rich, the soldiers, and the Loyalists live. Those who do no fight for scraps. Those who are not subject to the lottery. Those who do not have to look again and again into the eyes of those who they have raised and see the bleak, unending acceptance of their own deaths. They live there in their warm homes, their bellies full, laughing and happy, while we work unending hours to see to their comfort and needs. Pushing my anger down deep, I made my way down the well-worn path, careful to be unseen. If I'm found outside the city limits, I'll be killed and there will be no one after today to care for my two younger sisters.

Staying to the shadows, I quietly made my way past the markings that tell you only death awaits if you dare to cross and to the nearest house. Climbing over the debris, I slid between the houses and into the streets. Careful to avoid the outstretched hands and ignore the darkly whispered words, I quickly made my way home. Coming to my block, I could see the familiar faces of my neighbors gathered around the fires as they offered their good-byes to their friends and family. Making arrangements for their young in preparation for tonight's lottery. A lottery my cousin Rose is in. The last of my family besides my sisters. Rose has been my sister more than anything else, banding with me to ensure that we all had food. Her last older brother's lottery was a year past and now her turn had come. Unlike others, she will leave no young behind. Even the president's warning would not allow her conscience to give that fate to a child.

Holding back my tears, I stood at the threshold of our shabby home as the reality hits that after today I will never see her again. It will just be me trying to keep the young alive. Alive long enough to work, reach their own lottery, then die. Slamming my hand against the frame of the door, I raised my face to gaze upon the inky darkness above, wondering yet again if it would not just be best to smother them in their sleep and then take my own life. Is there any point to this, was there any point to anything?

"Misty, what are you doing?" Rose asked from behind me.

Wiping a hand over my face and pasting a smile on, I said, "I forgot my key, Rose."

Turing around, I see Josie and Tina are with her. Stepping back, I motion for her to open the door, sliding the key I palmed in my hand back into my pocket.

Waiting for them all to enter, I stepped in behind them and locked the door. Even in your own home you had to be careful. Making my way to the living room, I eased myself down onto the couch, allowing my eyes to latch on to the clock. Two hours. In two hours, another member of my family would be dead. In two hours, we would stand in front of the gates to the Cavern of Death. A place where none had ever entered and returned. The rituals of death were no longer observed; the only reason I even knew of them were from an Elder named Crowley. Long ago, the Elders that had won the first lottery had decided to be a living memory of our culture from the time before the darkness, when we walked upon the land and not under it. It was the only gift they could give to our people that the government could not take from us, the truth of our past. A secret hidden so well that only few outside the Elders knew the truth, for fear that the government would burn them as they had all books of the past to keep the truth hidden.

"Josie, Tina, go to your rooms. I need to talk to Misty for a moment," Rose said, breaking into my thoughts.

Taking a seat next to me on the couch, Rose pleaded, "Misty look at me." She forced me to take my gaze from the clock to hers. I couldn't deny her this, even though it was killing me. "I should have listened to you," she whispered, forcing me to fight back my tears.

I didn't need to ask what she meant, because I had been saying it for years. Years before her brothers went to their deaths, when our cousins stilled lived. Yes, she should have listened, they all should have listened. We should have left. Before her first brother went to the Cavern of Death, I begged them to leave, to head into the unexplored fissures and try to find a way to the surface. They told me it was foolish and that nothing remained above. The surface of our world was destroyed, a barren wasteland where nothing could survive. I had yelled back that though we may find death above, death here was certain. That here there was no escape from it.

Careful to keep my face blank, I turned to face her, allowing none of my hope to show. "Will you listen to me now, Rose?" I asked.

"No, Misty, it's too late for me," she said, grabbing my arm before I could turn away. "But it's not too late for you and the girls."

Wrenching my arm from her grip, I buried my face into my hands, trying to reign in my anger. "Are you so much a coward that you would rather die than take a chance at life?" I hissed, unable to hold my words back.

"Not a coward, no, but a realist. They already know about me and will search if I do not go to the cavern!" she yelled, causing me to jump. Rose didn't yell. Rose never lost her temper. "Now listen to me. I have spent these last two years gathering information," she said. Seeing my confusion, she lowered her voice, knowing she had my attention. "It's the reason I took the job in the factory Secretary division," she finished in a whisper, closing her eyes as a shudder raked her body. Seeming to shake the memories from her mind, she rose from her seat and went to her room.

Oh god, she had worked there for us. I had been so ashamed of her when she told me she had taken that job. It was a place of traitors. Those who accepted food and money, among other things, in exchange for informing on their own people and attending "events" in the other communities that stole pieces of your soul. The only thing that saved her from being a total outcast among our community was the memory of her brothers. For the memory of them alone, people did not snub her completely, but kept a wary distance.

The turmoil of my thoughts rolled through my head as she reentered the room carrying a portable vid display and a metal box. Placing them on the table in front of me, she moved around the room, pulling the curtains, making sure none could see inside. With timid hands, I reached forward and opened the box, shocked at what I saw— paper. What was Rose doing with paper? I had never seen paper outside of a picture during our schooling until age thirteen before we were sent to the factories to work. Running my fingers across it, I was amazed at the feel. I was so absorbed, I jumped a little when she came next to me and snatched the paper from the box and began unfolding it.

"I was unable to take this before today, but with everyone that will not be returning, even if it is missed they won't know who took it," Rose said nervously, as she spread it open. Taking a look at it, I couldn't help the shocked gasp that left my lips.

"Where"—I cleared my throat—"where, how did you find this?" I asked, still unable to believe what I was seeing, a map of the caverns.

"I found it in a long forgotten and sealed section of the main building. I don't think any have entered it in years judging by how thick the dust was." Turning to me, she gave me the first real smile I had seen from her in years.

"This is how you're going to find your way out. This map is an original map of the caverns. It shows every entrance to the caves that the original survivors used."

Standing up, I pulled her into my arms, hugging her as tightly as I could. We were both laughing and giggling so loudly that the girls came to see what we were doing. Stepping in front of the table to block their view, I waited until Rose shooed them back to their rooms before turning back to study the map. Kneeling down, I looked closely, shocked at what I was seeing. The cavern system was massive, more so than any could have imagined. How could we not have known this?

"You see it, too, don't you?" Rose asked, kneeling down across from me.

Shaking my head, I asked, "How is this possible that no one has ever suspected? There must be a hundred caverns." Raising my eyes to look into hers, I let the anger I felt course through me. "The whole purpose behind the lottery is population control, due to lack of space. The reason for it was that there are only four caverns and each class has their own cavern." Not that the other classes were forced into the lottery—no, they were allowed to control their breeding, while we were forced to breed for a young, strong workforce!

I saw matching anger in her eyes. "There's more, so much more than you can imagine. These caverns are not empty," she said, her hand sweeping the map, "but filled with our people." Seeing the confusion in my eyes, she pulled out the vid display. "The truth is here. Not all of it, but enough that if it is was discovered that we had it, every man, woman, and child in this cavern would be killed to keep this secret."

Before I could ask her what was in there, it sounded. The sound of her death rang through the cavern. It was a long, seemingly unending sound. The silence after such a sound was deafening. The time had come. The weeping of small children could be heard through the walls as they begged their family members not to leave them. Looking into Rose's eyes, all I saw was acceptance and it angered me, just as the acceptance that I had seen in everyone's eyes on this day had angered me. Why accept death? Why not fight for life? Rose had discovered something that no one had before and instead of wanting to know the truth for herself, she gives it to me and walks meekly to her death. Before I could give voice to my anger,

13

Josie and Tina walk in the room silencing it in my throat. Quickly, I gathered the box and vid display into my arms, taking them to my room, while Rose held the weeping girls as they tearfully say their good-byes.

By the time I rejoined them, Rose had managed to silence their cries. Nodding to me over their heads, I knew it was time. Walking to the door, I waited for the subdued group to join me before venturing out of our home into the large crowd that was making its way through the soldier-lined street. It is required that every person attend the lottery, with no exceptions. As we approached, I could hear the metal grating sound echo as the doors were opened to admit their next victims. I sighted the doors as we crested the hill and my heart beat accelerated as the impenetrable blackness of the cavern stared back at me. In a daze, I followed the crowd, letting it lead me where it will. A hand latched on to me, causing me to jerk as my eyes wildly searched for its owner and finally settled on Tristian. He pulled me closer to him, while his father, the Elder Crowley, moved to my other side, grounding me in the moment.

Tristian and Crowley moved us through the crowd to catch up with my family. I pressed my body into

Tristian in a way I had never done before, causing him to stiffen in surprise, but I needed the comfort as I tried to bury the fear coursing through me. The fear of a future without Rose and all the responsibilities that came with it. Finally reaching the cavern, I stepped forward to embrace Rose, giving her everything in that hug that I couldn't give her in words. With one last look, I pulled the girls off her with Tristian's help and took them to the section that we were to watch from. With dead eyes, I looked to the stage set just to the side of the cavern as the governor of our cavern stepped to the podium to give his speech. Our beloved president couldn't be bothered to deal with the lottery, but appointed a governor to deal with the Contributors.

The fat, balding man who stepped to the podium disgusted me. Having never missed a meal, the glow of health in his cheeks showed in the dim light. As a member of the Elite Caverns, he was given the best of everything— food, clothing, and education.

"Welcome, contributors" he said, in his high-pitched voice. As if we had a choice. "Today is a day of great joy, as you are chosen to journey into the Cavern of Death. But before we begin, let us remember why we stand here. Welcome Senator Peloci, whose father was one of the original signers of the treaty." He clapped his hands as a stern, bird-faced woman stepped forward.

Gazing out at us with unseeing eyes and a look on her face as if she smelled something rotten, she took the governor's place at the podium. "As was written in the treaties of peace, so it shall be. We who once roamed upon the earth in the light were forced into the darkness by the traitors—those who refused to do their duty to society and gave up their earnings and properties. Their greed led us to this. Those who tried to force their benevolent government for change and ended up causing the destruction of the world above, forcing us into the darkness below. In an act of mercy, the government forgave the traitors and allowed them to live in peace in the caverns as long as they took the place that they had refused in the world above. As we were forced to sacrifice and be banished to the world below, so shall the traitors know sacrifice. In the twenty-first year of their birth they must journey to the Cavern of Death and give up their lives so that those they had refused to provide for may live. This is how they will show that they regret their treason and the lives lost. As always, the government gave mercy where none should be given and decided to allow one hundred freedom from the Cavern of Death. Let these who age show testament to the government's benevolence and mercy. Let these who age be a testament to what you have destroyed in your greed. Today we remember your treason and our government's rebirth." She finished with a fanatical gleam in her eyes, her chin up high and a twisted look on her face that must pass as a smile, her stern voice still echoing her last words.

With an owl-like look, the governor hurried to her, nervously eying the crowd. That was not the approved speech and he was obviously worried about the reaction. "Thank you Senator Peloci. Without further ado, let us read the list of the one hundred," he hurriedly said, clumsily waving to his secretary, who stepped forward to drone out names as he led the arguing senator from the stage to her transportation. The names droned on as I listened desperately to each one, but the one I wished to hear was never said.

Emptiness filled me as I watched the governor take his place back at the podium, obviously wanting to be done. As the last name left the secretary's mouth, she was pushed to the side. "To those one hundred, rejoin your families and let the mercy of your government be shown. To the rest of you step forward now to begin your journey and know that your sacrifice today provides for all members of the caverns," he hurriedly finished, mopping his sweat-soaked, dripping forehead.

Numbness coursed through me. I kept my eyes on Rose's back as she stepped forward with the crowd, her name not among those pardoned from their fate. The crowd moved in utter silence. Not one looked back. Line after line stepped forward, disappearing into the darkness, never to be seen again.

Chapter 2

    If Tristian and his father had not been there, I don't know if we would have made it home. Gathering my sisters and me to them, they led us through the subdued crowd. When we reached our home, it was Tina who stepped forward and let us in, and without stopping, Tristian led me like a child to my room, helping me into my bed. Through the haze of my grief, I do not know how long he stayed with me before the sweet lull of oblivion claimed me. It was dark when I opened my eyes, but it was always dark. The temptation to remain where I was until death took me was great; only the knowledge that my sisters would be left alone forced me from my bed.

    With heavy limbs, I made my way to the kitchen. The smell of meat cooking, which was so rare, barely roused my appetite. I must have been in bed for more than a day if there was meat. The Contributors received meat once a year, two days after the lottery. Heavily armed trucks pulled into each square, allowing all families a portion. Their reward for the families' sacrifices. Sitting down at the table as the twins cooked, I was glad they did no more than smile their hello to me. I don't think I could have spoken at the moment, Rose's death still to raw within me. Quietly, they moved around the kitchen, bringing me water for my parched throat as they set the table for our feast. This was yet another way that the government controlled us. While people cried out for their family members that had been sacrificed, their bellies silenced them at the thought of not knowing hunger for a few moments. It was beyond cruel. While the ones to be sacrificed in the lottery dreaded the moment, their families secretly welcomed it because they knew that it brought meat. The guilt that those left behind had from delight forced them to not think of those that they lost, unable to bear the guilt.

These thoughts swirled in my head as Josie set my plate in front of me, causing what should be a delicious smell to turn rancid. Forcing myself to reach for the fork, I methodically brought the food to my lips. Again and again I repeated this, until nothing was left, all the while holding on to the hope that Rose had left me—the map. I would need my strength to save us. These thoughts were the only thing that let me keep what I had just eaten in my stomach. Rising from the table, I placed my dish into the sink before going to Tina and Josie. Embracing them both, I murmured, "Thank you, I'm going to lay down for a bit."

Softly closing the door to my room behind me, I slid the lock in place before prying up the loose board in the floor that hid my secrets. I took out the gifts that Rose had left while putting back the pieces of my family that I had kept to remember them. Memories of the past were too close to the surface to even look at the keepsakes, so I quickly turned my back to them while taking the map and vid display to my bed. Spreading the fragile paper map carefully across the bed, I let the enormity of what I was seeing sink in. The system of caverns were huge. Rose had said that our people were in them. How could this be? They never would have let so many of us live, we could easily overpower them and take control. I could understand her warning about them killing in order to keep it a secret. If this was common knowledge, if they were being forced to live as we live, serving them, it would cause a rebellion. Unfortunately that wasn't the only thing that didn't make sense. There was barely enough food, electricity, and supplies for us to survive on. How could there be enough to support all of this? Carefully searching the map, it took me a moment to find our cave, deep in the system, far back from the entrances originally used to enter the system those untold years ago. Most Contributors do not know how many generations have passed with us living below. The government does not teach this in the schools, keeping it a carefully guarded secret. I believe the Elders know, but when I asked Crowley he changed the subject.

Pushing these thoughts aside, I searched the map, trying to find other ways out. It showed smaller caves leading toward the surface that were marked unstable, caved in, or abandoned. None of these could be accessed through our cavern. To find a way out, I would need to get us into the other caverns. Caverns where people like us were forbidden to enter on penalty of death. Not just our own deaths, but the deaths of our whole family line. The only time Contributors left this cavern was when we went to the Cavern of Death. Other than during that time, we were born here, lived here, and worked here, never to see anything else beyond this cavern unless you were a Secretary and then you were watched at all times until you were returned. A knock at my door startled me from my thoughts. Grabbing the bed cover, I threw it over the map and vid display before going to the door. Taking a deep breath while I turned the lock, I cracked the door open and was startled to see Tristian.

"I came to check on you," he said, a small smile playing on his lips that didn't reach his eyes.

Staring at him, I made a decision that I hoped was right. Opening my door, I stepped back and waited for him to enter. After a small hesitation, he stepped over the threshold, moving into the room. Closing the door, I could see my sisters peeking around the corner. Shaking my head, I asked, "They went and got you, didn't they?"

Not bothering to pretend that he didn't know what I was talking about, he said, "They're worried," the look on his face telling me he was, too.

I nodded my head that I understood, because I did. If they were acting like this, I would be dragging them from the house, forcing them to get on with their lives. Moving past him, I folded my arms around myself as I tried to find the words to begin with. Turning to face him, I looked—I mean really looked—at him. Now that Rose was gone, he was my best friend. We had played together since we were children. I had loved knowledge and soaked it up like a sponge and his father was the keeper of knowledge, happy to give me what I sought. His friendship with my father made it impossible to deny me. After my parents' deaths, he watched out for my family, making sure that we never went hungry, that we never begged for death to escape the cold. Yes, Tristian would keep my secret, and more importantly, his father Crowley would do anything he could to help us, to ensure that he did not lose his son to the Cavern of Death. Between what Rose left behind and the knowledge of the Elders, I would have a real chance to save my family.

"I need your word, Tristian, on the life of your father, that what I'm about to show you, tell you, you will never tell another," I said, the seriousness of my words echoed in my tone. From the look on his face I could see I had insulted him, but that could not stop me—this was for the safety of my sisters.

His dark eyes flashed with his anger before he nodded his head. "You have my word, on the life of my father," he pushed out in a clipped tone.

Taking a deep breath, I nodded my head back and made my way to the bed, quickly pulling back the cover before I could change my mind. Turning my head to look at him, I watched as confusion turned to amazement. Not sparing me a glance, he walked up to the bed and carefully turned the map to face him. I could tell the exact moment he realized what he was looking at—his eyes grew round and his breath gasped before he shut all emotion behind a mask that even I couldn't penetrate.

"How did you get this?" he demanded, ripping his gaze from the map to bore into mine. If I had not seen that moment of fear flash in them before he masked it, I might have been afraid.

Climbing onto the bed, I motioned for him to join me. "Rose gave this to me. She stole it from a forgotten room in the government center." Reaching forward and taking his hand, keeping my eyes to his, I said, "She stole this so we can escape. I refuse to give my sisters to the Cavern of Death." I announced this, waiting for his reaction.

He sharply nodded his head and tightened his hand in mine, releasing it before saying the words I hoped to hear: "So, how do we get out of here?"

I was so relieved when he said those words I had to close my eyes to hold back the tears. I wasn't alone, he was going to go with me. When I opened my eyes, my feelings must have been there to read. With a crooked smile that had charmed more than half the girls in the caverns, he asked, "You didn't really think I'd let you go alone, did you?"

Gasping out a breath, I threw myself forward, wrapping my arms around him, my relief so great that my body trembled from it. Gaining some control, I pulled back and looked at him with a smile I couldn't contain. What I saw in his face wasn't an answering smile but a brooding look that he gazed at me with when he wasn't aware that I could see him. Ignoring it as I always did, I pulled out of his arms and sat back on my side of the bed. Reaching for the map between us, I turned it to face him, wanting to draw his thoughts back to our escape. "Tristian, look at the map and tell me what you see," I demanded, tapping my finger to the paper in front of us. After what seemed like forever, I felt his eyes leave me to gaze down at the map. Careful to hide my relief, I waited for him to see what Rose and I had saw. Taking a quick glance up to his face, I saw the wrinkle appear between his eyes as it did whenever he was in deep thought. Looking back to the map I waited.

I watched as his hand reached out and grazed out over the map. "That's not possible," he whispered, even as the truth of what he saw crowded his mind. "How could they have hidden this?" he asked, not expecting an answer, just speaking his thoughts out loud. After a few more minutes, he got up from the bed angrily, pacing the small confines of my room before turning on his heels to come and stand before me. Reaching out, he gripped my shoulders with bruising hands, pulling me from the bed to stand before him. "Do you understand what you have found?" he hissed, shaking me in his anger. Pushing me back onto the bed he turned his back to me, walking to the door. Jumping up, I lunged for him, wrapping my hand around his arm, forcing him to turn and face me. I needed him. I couldn't let him leave.

What showed in my face was something I couldn't control. It was something that I couldn't hide, fear. "Please don't leave, let's talk about this. I understand your anger, I feel it, too, but there is more that you need to know," I said desperately, hoping to stop him. It took a few moments of pleading before I could see a change in his face that told me he wasn't going to leave. "Rose told me more, not much, but I think you should know." Keeping him in my sight, I went back to the bed, waiting until he joined me. Locking my eyes with his, I said, "These caverns, they aren't empty," waiting to judge his reaction.

When he still hadn't said anything, I started to get worried, until he rolled his eyes. "So what, are the filled with Loyalists, military?" he asked, annoyed.

Shaking my head, I whispered, "No, they're filled with Contributors," afraid that in the silence of the room my voice would carry.

Ripping his eyes from mine, he glued his gaze to the map. I knew that he was doing the math. If each cavern held even a portion of our own population, then for the first time in centuries we outnumbered the takers. "Rose couldn't tell me much, but she said that some of the answers were on the vid disc that she smuggled out," I said, pointing to the small vid display on the bed. "I haven't looked at it yet," I told him, before he could ask.

Moving the map to the side, he sat on my bed and reached for the vid display. After a moment it came on. I took a seat next to him, turning my attention to the screen, wishing I had never looked.

A dark-haired man dressed in a white coat came on the screen. "This is Professor Clark Head of the relocation and mapping division of Trek Corp. As the Board is aware, the war is not going as we anticipated and at the request of the government we have been looking at alternative locations for population survival. In this search we have discovered a large cavern system project name Mammoth. As you can see by this digital display of the system, it is so large we have yet to map it completely; the density of the rocks will not allowing for sonic scans so we have had to manually view each location. So far we have discovered four hundred and sixty-two caves large enough to house one hundred thousand survivors each, not including smaller caves that can take anywhere from five thousand to twenty thousand each. There are four ways to enter this system large enough for mass entrance. The distance under the ground will allow protection from the atomic weapons fallout that is predicted to occur should we not be able to subdue the insurrection led by the rebel Contributors. It is our belief that this is the best chance we have of saving a portion of the population from extinction. Preparations have already began for animals, plants, and supplies to be moved into these caverns here and here, to test long-range growth suitability. Theses caverns being so large, we have turned them into multi-floor units that will allow for continued growth of our supplies. A full report is being sent along with recommendations on when to start the evacuation of the surface prior to the government's last stand contingent known as Revelation."

The screen went blue before it started again, the date appearing at the bottom was two years later. A man with a large scar down his cheek and a marbled eye in a military uniform appeared. "The Rebel Terrorists have taken control of most of the states. They currently have the capitol surrounded, unaware that the president and government officials have already been moved to the Mammoth Project. It is our belief that we cannot hold them back from success and Revelation should be deployed. Loyalists and their families have already been moved to the safety of the caves. It is my recommendation that Revelation is launched in these Sections first," he said, pointing to a map behind him. "The other Sections here and here hold the Rebels' woman and children in large numbers and should be saved until we can extract enough for the required workforce and breeding programs. The distance from the blasts should assure that the stock is not contaminated by radiation or damaged in any other significant way before they can be moved underground. Also the strongest of the men are currently surrounding the capitol—these are the stock we will wish to take. As discussed, once they are informed of the coming death of the surface of this planet, they will negotiate to save their women and children and will agree to the government demands. If my instructions have changed, contact me immediately or we shall proceed with operation Revelation."

Again the screen went blue before coming back on. When it started this time, twenty years had passed. A dark-haired woman in a lab coat now stood in front of us. "The disease that has swept the livestock was not controlled in time and has spread to the other livestock areas and all animals are now infected, they are either dying or dead. The meat is unusable; the test subjects that we had ingest it were dead within forty-eight hours. The disease seems to only affect humans through digestion and is not a worry for widespread epidemic. Cloning of the animal DNA has not been successful. They do not reach majority before the virus, which we can only assume is airborne, infects them. We have tried without success to inoculate against the virus. We can only assume that the caves' core temperature and environment are a perfect host for this disease. This avenue as a food source has been lost to us. Stocks of inventory have been checked and it has been determined that there is a one-year supply of protein remaining before it is exhausted. Alternatives must be reviewed, please advise."

Two years later, the same doctor appeared on the screen. "We have been informed by our liaison that the rioting in the rebel caves have reached dangerous proportions. The lack of food from overpopulation and

31

limited supplies is causing a mass rebellion that we are afraid will cause them to discover the other rebel caves and unite them against us. We believe we have found a solution. Though we keep the Rebels for their ability to do the work and to maintain the maintenance of our infrastructure and daily life, we have found that it is the Elders of their group that are causing the outbreaks of rebellion. The Elders also do not have the strength or stamina to work the fourteen-hour days without damages occurring within their bodies. While we can mend the damages, we believe that this is a waste of our resources and after a certain age they are no longer even good for work and become a nonproducing drain on our resources. After careful discussion we believe that we have come up with a solution to ensure a manageable population, a young, strong workforce and a limitless food supply. Detailed in my report are our recommendations, we await your reply."

Two months later, the same doctor appeared. "We are glad to hear that the rebellion has been put down and that our recommendations were followed and placed in the new treaty. In preparation of your agreement with our plan, a new prototype processing plant is already under construction and will be operational before the first harvest. Details on what will be needed at each cavern so that they have their own processing plant are being drawn up. We believe that the first harvest will yield enough meat to give us a five-year surplus. All information on minimum rebel population maintenance is being sent to you including Loyalist growth figures for the next ten years. We shall continue to monitor the food supply and give recommendations for any vaccines or nutrients we believe are needed."

I stared at the blue screen with vacant eyes as the words of that long-dead monster faded in the silent room. I don't know how long we sat there before the knock on the door startled me from my thoughts. Moving like in a dream, I took the vid display from Tristian's limp fingers and placed it on the bed with the map, pulling the covers over it. Standing up, I walked to the door and opened it to a worried Josie. Blinking at me like an owl, she opened her mouth a few times before the words finally escaped. "I'm sorry to bother you, but it's been hours and I just wanted to make sure you were alright," she said, worry clear in her tone. Unable to answer her, I just stared until she nervously started to fidget. "I can see that you guys are busy, I just wanted to let you know that there's meat still on the stove if ..."

Not letting her finish, I pushed her out of the way and dashed for the bathroom, barely making it. There I stayed until I had nothing left to give, until my groans turned to heaves, until my heaves turned to sobs.

Chapter 3

I could hear my sisters' sobs echo through the silent house. Siting in the living room, they drown me. Through the bedroom door, they flow down the stairs, creating rivers of sorrow. I know my sisters are afraid that I've gone insane. I want to assure them that I haven't, but how can I assure them of something I'm not sure of myself? Yesterday, when I finally dragged myself from the bathroom, I went into the kitchen for a glass of water and found them eating the meat and I snapped. Grabbing their plates, I threw them at the wall. The pan that held the rest followed. Terrified, they tried to restrain me and I snapped, smacking at them. Seeing Tristian in the doorway, they ran to him for help, but he just looked on with a vacant stare before he turned and quietly and left. Their fear fed my anger as I destroyed the kitchen. The sounds of my rage echoed as they cowered by the door in fear, watching my madness before turning to flee to their room.

Now, a day later, I still sat in the same spot I collapsed in yesterday like a statue, trying to come to terms with what I learned. Did Rose know what they were going to do to her when she went to that cavern? Oh, if there is any mercy left in our world, please don't let her have known. Don't let her have known that we are cattle raised and butchered. Don't let her have thought of her brothers, her parents, and her friends being served to us as a special treat for being good little cows who walked into the slaughter house. Once a year we were given meat as a remembrance of the treaties, of the sacrifices that we were forced to make. How they must laugh at us as they fed us our loved ones.

These thoughts lead to madness, and as much as I wished that it would take me so that I could forget what I now knew, I couldn't let it. My sisters needed me. Rising from the chair, I made my way up the stairs to their door, carefully knocking. "Josie, Tina, I'm going out. I don't want you to worry. I'm OK now. I'm going to see Tristian. I'll be home soon, I love you," I told the closed door, unwilling to open it and face what I did. Gathering my coat, I walked out the door, careful to lock it behind me. It must be later than I thought, workers were wearily making their way through the streets back to their homes. That was another problem I would have to deal with soon, none of us had been to work since the lottery. While I made sure we had spare rations, they wouldn't last us long and the only way to receive new rations was to work. Another way they controlled us. You couldn't buy rations, you had to work in the factories for the gray slop they called food.

Nodding my head at the familiar faces I passed, I quickly made my way to Tristian's. I was surprised when I turned the corner to his house and saw several Elders entering. While the Elders met, they were always careful about it not wanting to raise the government's suspicions. Stepping back before I was seen, I retraced my steps until I found the alley that would take me to the back of Tristian's home. Quietly making my way to his window, I gazed in and saw that the room was empty. Opening it, I climbed in like we use to do as children, then made my way quietly to his door, cracking it open to hear what was going on.

"Crowley, you know our laws, those one hundred that survived the lottery are to be brought into the fold. It is the way it has always been. This is how we maintain a living memory for our people," Elder Gillon said, his exasperation clear.

"And I tell you, Gillon, that there is something very wrong. The lottery this year was different. I think we need to watch those who were chosen and make sure that they are who they are supposed to be," Elder Crowley said.

"Who they are supposed to be?" Gillon scoffed. "Listen to yourself, you sound insane. What I think is that you are seeing shadows where there are none."

"Gillon, I agree with Crowley, this lottery was different. That woman they brought in, there was something very strange going on," Elder Parks interjected.

"You, too, Parks? Are you going to support Crowley in this lunacy? What of you, Terris? Where do you stand?"

"I agree that there is no harm in waiting until we are sure that everything and everyone is who they say, Gillon," Terris said to the silent room.

"Fine, we will call a meeting of the Elders to have a ruling," Gillon announced, before walking out.

"What's on your mind, Crowley?" Elder Terris asked as soon as Gillon was gone.

"There is something wrong. I do not think having a council meeting would be a good idea. I think that's what they're waiting for, a reason to say we were plotting and to wipe us out," he declared.

"We'll begin investigating the new lottery winners and try to hold off Gillon from calling a council meeting, my friend," he said. The mummer of good-byes warned me to close the door.

"You can come out now, Misty," sounded a voice in the house, starling me. Looking toward the window, I discarded the idea of sneaking out and went out the door to face a weary Crowley.

"How is it that you always know?" I asked, smiling at the thought of all the times he caught us sneaking in.

Shaking his head, he motioned for me to take a seat. "It's a parent thing, I have a sixth sense for you children when you're doing something you're not supposed to," he replied, with a small twist of his lips. "Now, do you want to tell me what has happened with Tristian? I mean, he is the reason for your visit." He sighed, pointing to the seat across from him.

Not bothering to deny it, I asked, "Is he here?" I sat down, feeling just a weary as he looked.

"No, he went out early in the day and hasn't been home since. He was quite occupied with something on his mind and needed time to think," he replied, looking at me expectantly.

Not ready to share my secrets and give him the answers he sought, I said, "I've asked you this before and you've never answered." Seeing that I caught his interest, but his smile telling me he knew I was changing the subject, I quickly asked, "How long have our people been here in the caves?" The hoped-for answer had taken on new meaning for me.

For a long time he stared at me, so long I didn't think he was going to answer. So when he spoke I jumped a little. "No one is truly sure. The best answer that I can give you is around three thousand years, but I believe that it has been longer, but by how much I don't know."

Starting slowly, I said, "I know that the world above us was destroyed, but after so long could it have..." I grasped for the right word. "Could it have repaired itself? Could there be life there again?" I finished, unable to think how else to word it.

"I'm not a scientist, Misty, I don't know if it could repair itself."

Suddenly I was not so tired. "That's not what I asked, Crowley, do you *think* that it could have repaired itself?"

"Yes, I think that it could have repaired itself," he answered, smiling softly. "I think that nature may have had to bend to our will but it did not break."

I nodded my head in relief. "Has anyone ever gone to check to see if the surface was livable again?" I asked, trying to hide my excitement.

"That I know of, no. No one has been to the surface since the tunnels were sealed after we entered all those centuries ago." Leaning forward, he asked, "Misty, why all these questions?"

Staring at him, I made my decision. "Hypothetically, if you could take Tristian to the surface and escape the lottery, would you?"

"Yes," he said, no hesitation in his words.

"Even not knowing if there is anything up there to escape to?"

"I'd take him anyway. Better he died up there free than a slave to the system here," he answered with venom, hating as much as I the hopelessness of it all.

"I feel the same way for my sisters," I whispered, choked with emotion. "What if I told you that there is a map of the caverns?"

"I would say that is a very dangerous thing to have," he said slowly, sitting up a little straighter at my words.

"And hypothetically, what if this map showed hundreds of caves? Caves filled with Contributors who knew nothing about each other?" I finished, looking in his eyes so he could see the truth of my words.

His sharp indrawn breath was loud in the silent room. As I watched his eyes, I saw the possibilities this knowledge brought flash through them. A key turning in the lock broke our connection, causing us both to turn and watch the door in apprehension. Relief flooded the room when Tristian walked in. "Sorry I'm late, Dad. I had some things to do, how about we"—he stopped mid-sentence, surprise flashing in his eyes when he saw me. Nodding his head to me he turned cautious eyes to his father.

"Son, come in and sit. Misty and I were having a hypothetical discussion. Why don't you join us?" he said, breaking the awkward silence, but increasing the Tristian's tension.

I made room on the small couch next to me, and Tristian stiffly sat down. "How much have you told him?" he asked.

"Some, not all," I replied, not bothering with pretense.

"I thought we agreed to tell no one," he growled, his anger clear. Not because he didn't trust his father, but because he knew the danger of the knowledge we had.

"Your father has information we need," I said, reaching out and taking his hand. I waited until he looked at me. "And you never would have left without telling your father good-bye," I whispered, pleading with my eyes to help him understand why we had to share this burden with his father. When I felt his thumb glide across my hand, I knew I was forgiven because he knew I was right.

"Where did you get this information?" Crowley asked, breaking in.

"Rose gave it to me before the lottery. She became a Secretary to gather information so I could escape with my sisters," I told him, pride and sorrow clear in my voice.

"Why wouldn't she bring it to me?" Crowley muttered.

"What do you mean? Why would she bring it to the Elders? She was a Secretary, an outcast," I said, confused as to why he would think she would bring it to the people who scorned her.

Indecision played in his eyes before he answered me. "Your cousin was part of an infiltration group trying to gather information on the government and the caverns. She was the best we had. No one knew that she was an operative other than myself and one other Elder. It was safer for her this way. We believe that there have been government plants among the Elders since the conception of the lottery, feeding them information that have gotten many of our best agents killed. Your cousin was working with us to stop the lottery and force the government to see us as equals," he finished, staring at me in complete earnest belief of his cause.

I laughed. I couldn't help it. Not a little giggle, but a full-blown laugh of hysterics. My Rose had a secret life. A life that risked every member of our family and she never told me. My best friend. The hand that struck me wasn't light. Shocked, I brought my hand to my cheek and turned large eyes to Tristian, who stood in front of me holding me by my upper arms, concern clear on his face. Releasing one arm, he brought a gentle finger to my face, wiping away tears I didn't realize I was shedding. Turning my head to a concerned Crowley, I couldn't help the scorn that entered my voice. "Do you want to know why Rose didn't bring you what she found?" When all he did was shake his head, it released the flood gate of emotion that I had been holding back. Wanting to lash out and hurt someone as I hurt, I said, "She didn't bring it to you because you think you can force the government to see us as equals. To them we are about as equal as a bug under your shoe. You see, they will never see us as equals because they don't want their main course sitting at their table talking, but well-seasoned and on their plates." I laughed cruelly, pulling my arm from Tristian before sitting back on the couch and hugging myself. I felt no better at the pain he was about to know made worse at the harshness of my delivery.

"I don't understand. What are you saying? You're not making sense!" he shouted. Confused and not getting an answer from me, he turned to Tristian. "What is she talking about?" Crowley demanded.

Sighing, Tristian sat down next to me and motioned for his father to retake his seat. When he reached over to take my hand, I shoved it under my armpit and scooted over as far as I could away from him. "Did you know?" I asked, having to know the truth. His silence was answer enough that my two only friends had lied to me. If they lied to me about this, what else were they keeping secret from me? Did I really ever know either of them? "How long?" I asked again.

"How long what, Misty?" he wearily asked.

Turning my head to face him, I gritted out through my teeth, "How long was Rose part of whatever this is?"

With a closed expression, he stared into my eyes. "Since before her brothers went to the Cavern of Death. They were the members who brought her in."

Nodding my head once that I understood, I dismissed him and turned to look at Crowley. Pushing down my emotions, I focused my dead gaze onto him. "To answer your question, Rose gave me two things: a map and a vid disc, telling me that no one must ever know because it would put the whole cavern under a death sentence. She gave these things to me to help me escape to the surface with my sisters. Obviously I told Tristian and now I am going to tell you, but I need your word—for what it's worth—that for now everything will remain between the three of us." Receiving a nod, I continued. "There are over four hundred occupied caverns with populations ranging from five thousand to one hundred thousand each. These figures come from the vid disc that we watched. I'm not sure how many are occupied by Contributors, but Rose led me to believe most of them were. We also saw that it was the government, not the Contributors that set into motion the cleansing called the Revelation. They had lost and instead of accepting defeat, they destroyed the surface, forcing us to admit defeat or die above. Unfortunately that isn't the worst that the vid disc has shown us." Stopping to take a breath, I closed my eyes and hardened my heart to what I was about to say. "Twenty years after the destruction of the surface, the animals brought below sickened and died, greatly reducing the caverns' food sources. There were riots running rampant through the caverns. To hold control, the government brutally put the

Contributors down and forced them to sign a new treaty that solved all the government's problems. The new treaty took care of population control. It took care of the sick and old, allowing for a young workforce at all times"— stopping, I looked into Crowley's eyes, holding them to mine to make sure he understood what I was about to say— "and it took care of the food shortages because every year a new herd of cattle is butchered."

Shaking his head in confusion, he said, "I don't understand, you said that all of the animals died thousands of years ago. How could there still be meat?" Instead of answering him, I just stared at him, forcing him to accept the truth staring him in the face. Minutes passed and a hundred emotions flashed across his face before I saw the truth of my words sink in, followed by the horror its reality brings. "You're wrong," he whispered in despair, turning to his son. "Please tell me it's not true," he pleaded.

"I can't," Tristian softly answered before angrily swiping the stray tear that drifted down his cheek.

As mad as I was at Tristian and his father, I shared their grief and burden of this truth. Rising from the couch, I laid a gentle hand on Crowley before moving away. This was not something that needed to be shared. Each had to deal with this horror alone as they came to terms with their own guilt of what they had unwittingly done and what had been done to their children, families, and friends. Walking to the door, I quietly let myself out, wondering if any of us would ever come to terms to with what had been done in the shadows of the Cavern of Death.

Chapter 4

By the time I got up in the morning, Josie and Tina were gone. A quickly left message in the kitchen stated that they had gone to work at the fabric factory for their shift and would return later. I knew they were avoiding me, having feigned sleep when I had returned last night so they wouldn't have to speak to me. The silence of the house was unsettling. I was rarely home alone, so I never realized how quiet it could be. Was this how it was when you were the last member of your family? Was this what they came home to until it was their time to enter the Cavern of Death? If it was, I could imagine that they looked at the cavern in relief, knowing that they wouldn't be going back to their empty homes. That they finally had an end to the madness that the unending silence brought.

The knock on the door wasn't loud, but echoed through the lifeless house. Going to it, I was careful to stay to the side and remain unseen as I peeked through the curtain to see who was there. Unsurprised at my visitor, I unlocked the door. Opening it enough for him to enter, I stepped to the side and waited. After a moment's hesitation, he crossed the threshold and I silently closed it and relocked it, trying to keep the world at bay. Moving past him, I went to the living room, not bothering to see if he followed, and took a seat. The silence stretched in the small room, until he broke and said what he came here to say: "I would like to see the vid disc that you spoke of."

"Wait here," I said, before rising and retrieving it from its hiding spot. Opening the vid display, I brought up the video, pausing it before it could begin. Walking to his side, I placed it in his outstretched hands. "Just press play," I murmured, before resuming my seat across from him. We both sat in silence as the words began to fill the empty void of the room. I didn't need to watch it again; it was seared into me so as its words reached me, its accompanying images played back in my mind. As the last word left that evil woman's mouth and the room went quiet again, I had to fight down the nausea that had come with it.

"Tristian's lottery is next year," he croaked, trying to fight back his emotions. "I can't let him go to the lottery. You will take him with you."

"Yes," I stated. It wasn't a question, but a fact. No matter how angry I was with him, I would never have left him behind to this fate.

"May I see the map? Rising from my seat, I took the vid display and returned a moment later with the map, spreading it out on the table in front of him. Pushing the table closer to him, I took a seat on the floor and waited. I had spent all last night trying to figure out the best route for us to take. Each route had its own dangers, ranging anywhere from cave-ins to soldiers and I didn't know which was worse. We could possibly kill a soldier, but could we dig ourselves out from a cave-in? "You'll have to cross the border into the Loyalist cavern to even begin to have a chance of reaching one of these exits, the military cavern is obviously not even an option. Have you thought of how you'll get the four of you across?" Crowley asked, as he frowned at the map in front of him.

Unfortunately, that is what I had spent the other half of the night trying to figure out. No one had ever made it across to another cavern, the security at the entrances making it impossible. The solution I had come up with was one I didn't want to have to use. Clearing my throat, I said, "I'm not sure if it's possible to make it into the Loyalist cavern with the military presence in front of it. Even if we made it past the first layer, I just don't know how many are posted on the other side."

He must have heard something in my voice that betrayed me. Raising his eyes, he focused on me. "From the reports our agents have told us, there are ten on rotation at all times with heavy weapons, but I think you had already realized it would be something like that. So entering through the Loyalists cavern isn't going to happen, which only leaves one choice."

"Yes, only one," I murmured.

Nodding his head, he dropped his eyes back to the map before continuing. "It's the smart choice. There are only two token guards patrolling there at any time. It's not exactly a place where anyone is rushing to enter. A small disturbance near there would draw the guards away long enough for you to enter. Since the remains aren't brought through our cavern, there must be an entryway into the Loyalist cavern. I doubt that their side is even guarded, but to be sure, I'll have an agent check the next time they are escorted across the border. Hopefully they'll be going in the direction of the Cavern of Death.

"That would be helpful, thank you," I told him, before discussing our next problem. "My sisters work in the fabric factory, so I have access to the cloth that is produced.

If I can obtain it, do you have anyone trusted that could produce us clothing to blend into the Loyalist section?"

"Your sisters are excellent seamstresses. Why not have them do the work?"

I loved my sisters, but I knew that they would ask questions that were better off not being answered for as long as possible. One wrong word even by accident could mean our deaths. "I would prefer to keep them in the dark about our plans for as long as possible," I said, instead of the truth, that I was afraid that they would rebel once they learned of our plans. They had always been afraid of the unknown, preferring the comforts of routine to give them a sense of stability in an otherwise unstable world.

Nodding his head in understanding at what I left unsaid, he said, "There is an Elder who I would trust to do the work." Seeing my objections, he held up his hand to stop me. "She is vetted for many years and I trust her. Remember this is also my son's life, I understand the risks."

The next few hours we spent going over every possible route and the issues involved with each. Finally we came up with three routes that would give us our best chance. The primary one, if we could reach it, would force us to cross three borders, but I agreed that it was worth the risk if we felt that we could make it. It was an actual sub-entrance originally used by the designers of our prison. While the means of transport they had originally used to get down here would be gone, the size of the shaft would more than make up for it. Our least favorite was in the Loyalist cavern. Partially explored and abandoned due to instability, it could be a death trap for unexperienced climbers like my sisters. I wasn't worried about Tristian or I; we were climbers from a young age, always looking to escape the poverty that surrounded us, finding little cracks we could slide through to explore. Josie and Tina would be our weak links in this journey, but ones I was willing to die to protect.

"How will we get the supplies and equipment unseen with us? I'm sure Loyalists don't walk around with climbing equipment, food, and water. It will be a dead giveaway that we don't belong," I said, voicing my thoughts.

Pondering our dilemma, Crowley responded, "We'll have to figure a way to conceal as much as we can under your clothing, and for the rest we'll have to design bags that look like they belong there." I nodded my head in agreement, it was the only option. "You'll wear your climbing suits under your clothing—it will save time if you're discovered and have to run for the fissure. The guards pursuing you will have bulky uniforms, making it harder to move in the tighter space."

With that sorted out, I moved to something I knew had to be said. "Eventually it will be noticed we are missing. One or two gone could have been an accident or a reckoning—no one will think too much of the bodies missing as it's happened before. The problem is with four missing and one being the child of an Elder. I heard what you said to the other Elders, that you believe there are government spies watching you. If you don't raise the alarm that Tristian is missing, they'll know for certain that something is wrong. They'll definitely take you in for questioning and if you tell them about the vid disc it could mean the life of every living soul in our cavern. I think it would be better if you come with us so there is no chance of them ever finding out," I concluded, hoping he would listen to reason. I should have known better.

Leaning back in the chair, he rubbed his hand across his face before he spoke. "Since my twenty-first year, my life has been about the devotion of our people's history and the sheer, unrelenting gratefulness that I was allowed to raise my child when so many others couldn't. Thinking I had received a gift instead of the curse that it truly was. A curse to watch all those you loved die and be left as a living memory to their lives. For twenty years, I have said good-bye to almost everything that has held true meaning in life. You children are the last pieces. I will gladly die before I give them what they want, but I've thought about this, too. Once you're out of this cavern you should be safe in the sense that there is no chance they will search anywhere else but here if I raise the alarm. Which may work in your favor if this cavern is the military's focus. I'm more selfish, also, for wanting to stay for revenge." Adding strength to his voice, he continued, "While I had acknowledged the deaths of my loved ones as something endured until we could bring change and freedom to our people, there is no way I can accept what was done to them and what they plan to do to my child. What they did to my wife. I'm an Elder, the keeper of the truth, and this is a truth that must be known. Now that I'm aware of the other caverns, I'll begin to gather those who can be trusted and show them the truth. If you four make it out unseen, then we may be able to use that as a way to access the other caverns to spread the word and unite with the other Contributors out there. What we have endured in the name of peace to ensure our race's survival is one thing, but these atrocities must be answered for. No government has the right to single out one people that is part of their sovereign rule. Again and again through our history we have been forced to endure their indifference to our suffering and hardships, whipped like an animal if we offered a word of protest. We are not inferiors, but what our country once stood for, the hardworking who built it. Who suffered gladly in silence knowing that their sacrifice would lead to a better life for their children. In a moment of desperation, we rebelled against the tyrants who thought themselves kings, stealing what we bled for to line their greedy pockets and spread our children's wealth to the takers of our society. Men and woman who laughed at our labors while spending their time trying to take more from us instead of going out and fighting for their own. The more they received, the greedier they became, selling their votes to a government that lavished them with more every election to keep them happy until the takers far outnumbered the Contributors. Oh, yes, we rebelled. The injustices so great against us we could no longer stand it. Not willing to lose control, they destroyed the surface of our world, sending us into hell. Blaming us for their misdeed. Know this, when we are united once more, there will be no treaty. We will not stand down. What was done cannot be forgiven. This time, when they lose, there will be no pit to flee to. If they wish to silence us, then they will join us in this tomb," he proclaimed, slamming his hand to the arm of the chair, chest heaving, and resolve etched in the grimness of his face.

Staring at him in this moment, I was awed by what I saw. This was no broken man that I had left the night before. This was a man unwilling to let the injustice of a flawed system steal any more from him. He had been pushed to all limits and instead of breaking, it had made him stronger. In that moment I felt that strength flow to me, empower me to believe that I could do this. I could lead us out of here. I could lead us out of the darkness and into the light.

Chapter 5

In the week that followed my talk with Crowley, I was a wreck. Every knock on our door caused my heart to race. Every face I passed on the streets I was certain was following me, waiting for me to make a move. Terrified, I hide my emotions deep, letting nothing show until it seemed like I was another person than the one that walked in our world just a short time ago. My sisters were afraid for me and of me, speaking in whispered tones whenever I was around. Their worried gazes followed my every move. Ignoring them because I knew that I couldn't allay their fears, I continued with the plan.

Sneaking into the fabric factory was more difficult than I thought. There had been guards stationed there during the night and I had been almost caught more times than I cared to count. Taking the fabric to Crowley was just as difficult. The morning I went to take the fabric to him, soldiers had lined the streets doing random house searches, checking for contraband, and they almost caught me with it. Only quick thinking and a convenient alley filled with debris saved me from being caught. Luckily, when I went back later that night, the fabric I had stashed in the alley was still there waiting for me. Sneaking it in through

Tristian's window, I was afraid to be seen entering their home. Watching the doors and windows, I sat in the living room to find out if they had any new information. "Have your agents found out if the cavern is guarded on the other side?" I asked lowly, not wanting my voice to carry.

Shaking his head, Crowley handed me a glass of water and sat down next to Tristian "No, they've been to the Loyalist cavern, but the house that they were taken to isn't deep into the cavern, but very near the border," he said, but the distracted look on his face told me that there was more. I didn't have long to wait before he continued. "There is something strange. We don't keep written reports because we are afraid of discovery, but I've been thinking a lot lately of the reports and have been speaking with the agents. Something that we have never connected before is now blatantly clear. They are never taken far into the Loyalist cavern, only near the edge and from what I've been able to put together, they are always taken to the same street."

"Maybe those houses are used as their meeting houses for when outsiders are brought in to control what they see and where they go," I concluded, thinking that made perfect sense.

"I was thinking the same thing, but as I spoke to the agents, they said that there were personal images of the party's hosts and their family around the houses. No, they are definitely personal residences," he said, taking a sip from his glass. "The other thing they noticed, now that I pointed it out, is that it isn't alive there." Seeing mine and Tristian's confusion, he said, "Here there is always noise, a sense of life if you will, but there they say beyond the sounds that come from that house, they rarely hear anything, not a child's cry, the sound of a footstep, nothing," Crowley finished, clearly disturbed.

Unfortunately, it disturbed me that the whole plan was to blend into the community, a community that should be alive and thriving without a care in the world. If the streets were empty, we would be spotted. How could a community as large as that one is supposed to be, be empty? It made absolutely no sense.

"They have to be mistaken or there is some sort of sound buffer," Tristian said, voicing my thoughts.

"I know none of it makes sense, Tristian, and that's the problem—even with a sound buffer, there would be some residual noise in a cavern that size," Crowley responded, before changing the subject. "The clothing will be ready in two days. On the third day, I want you all gone from here. There is something not right going on around here—the soldiers were acting strangely, they're targeting Elders' homes. I think I was right about our new lottery winners and the government has become suspicious as to why we haven't brought them into the fold yet. Gillon was pushing for a meeting of the Elders and it has been scheduled in three days' time. This will be the perfect distraction for you. While they are focused on us, you can make good on your plans."

"Dad, what type of trouble are you expecting?" Tristian asked, his concern clear.

"Nothing we haven't dealt with before," Crowley said, smiling and dismissing Tristian's concerns.

Realizing that he would say no more on it, I said, "It's agreed then, in three days we make our move." Rising from my seat, I said my good-byes and headed for Tristian's room. Moving to the window, I was stopped by a hand on my arm. "I need to get back home, Josie and Tina are waiting," I said.

"Josie and Tina are hiding from you," he retorted, "and they're who we have to talk about."

"My family is my business, Tristian, and it doesn't concern you," I hissed, trying to pull me arm free.

Tightening his grip, he swung me around, forcing me to land against his chest. Grabbing my chin, he gripped it and forced me to meet his eyes. "They are my responsibility, too, and I will be heard now," he growled, releasing my chin and dragging me to the bed. Throwing me against it, he said, "Sit."

Glaring at him the whole time, which seemed to amuse him, I moved myself up so my back could rest against the wall. "Go ahead," I sneered, waving my hand for him to begin.

With a smile on his face that I wanted to slap, he said, "My father filled me in on his talk with you and I agree that the Cavern of Death is most likely our best way through, but have you given any thought on what that could mean?"

"Yes, of course I've given it thought," I said. What did he think I had done every moment since I had seen that damn vid disc? It haunted my waking hours and dreams, causing me to wake with screams trapped in my throat as accusing dead stares flashed through my mind.

Shaking his head, he said, "I mean have you thought of what we might see in that cavern? What Josie and Tina might see?"

Were my dreams a prophecy of my future when I walked through that cavern? Would those dead stares follow my every move? I could already hear Josie and Tina's screams echoing in my head as they looked at Rose's lifeless, maimed body. I knew what he was saying, if I brought them in their unprepared, the horrors they might see would drive them insane, fracturing their fragile minds. I couldn't stop the sob that escaped my throat any more then I could stop Tristan when he gathered me into his arms. He was right, they had to be told and it was my place to tell them.

"No, not just your place—I'll be there with you to help them accept it," Tristan whispered into my hair, startling me as I realized I had been speaking my thoughts aloud.

"Why did you and Rose hide the truth from me?" I croaked through my tears.

"We did it to protect you. Had you known, you would have wanted to help and neither of us wanted you to experience the depraved acts that she and your cousins had in the name of freedom. You, for all your fierceness, are still pure, uncorrupted by the daily struggles of our lives. By keeping this from you, she saved a part of herself that would have been lost otherwise. Only with you was she ever the girl that she should have been, instead of the woman that she had to become," he said, so simply, as if it was the most natural conclusion to come to.

Sobs tore from my soul at his words. I was lost. Pushing into Tristan, I forced him down on the bed, curling myself onto his chest. Like a broken child, I sought comfort, burying my face, hiding from the world and the pains that it held. Sleep came quickly, as I was exhausted by the lack that I had since before Rose's death and the turmoil of my emotions, and I embraced its sweet oblivion when it came.

I've slept in Tristian's arms before, so I wasn't concerned when I woke in them. Careful not to awaken him, I slowly pulled myself free from his tight grip. Rising from the bed, I spotted my shoes that he must have removed and quietly put them on and made my way through the window, closing it silently after me. It was totally dark as I made my way home, telling me it was deep into the night. I don't know what alerted me that I wasn't alone, but a feeling shook me, causing me to blend deeper into the shadows and look carefully into the darkness. Spotting a slight movement, I froze and waited as two men dressed in dark clothing made their way through the streets away from me. There was something not right about them, something that didn't belong. Matching their stealthy movement, careful to stay out of sight, I followed them, surprised when they stopped at the Elder Gillon's home. After a moment, the door opened and they entered, a sliver of light peeking out to the night from the sealed house. Careful to keep to the shadows of the homes, I made my way to an alley near Gillon's home. Moving through it quickly, I made my way around to the back of his home, and crouching down, I moved under a cracked window so that I could hear the voices coming from inside.

"I'm doing the best I can," Gillon's voice screeched. "It's that bastard Crowley, he's the one that is holding the others back from the induction of the new members."

"Can you terminate him and take care of the problem without causing suspicion?" a raspy voice asked.

"It's best to wait until after their Council meeting. I have enough votes that I can get it passed, then I'll make sure that he causes no trouble for my replacement," he said, laughing evilly. "These people are such fools, it's hard to believe that their ancestors almost toppled the government. I can't wait to be away from the filth of this place. I was only supposed to be here for two years before a replacement was sent to take my place, and it's been five. I know that bastard Vincent was behind it!" he accused, a loud crash punctuating his words.

"You place too much importance on time, Jalic, and not enough on your mission. It was your duty to remain until you were no longer needed. I'm sure you're not questioning your superiors, are you?" the voice intoned. In a bored tone, the man continued, "The information that you have gathered on the Rebels has been useful. You should take it as a compliment that they allowed you to remain these last three years—it means that you have been effectual at your assignment. Now if you are done complaining, give me your vid disc with your reports so we may leave."

"Here, take it and hopefully the next time we meet it won't be in this hovel," Gillon barked. Fading footsteps and a slammed door announced that he left the room.

"Do you think he will be a problem?" the silent one asked, speaking for the first time.

"If he becomes a problem, his replacement will silence him permanently," the other answered, unconcerned.

No sound other than a soft click of the door told me they had left. As quickly and quietly as I could, I retraced my steps, barely catching sight of the direction that they went. Knowing that it was dangerous, I followed them anyway, through the twists and turns of the streets, careful to stay out of sight. I followed them all the way to the entrance of the Loyalist cave, where the soldiers parted to let them cross. Turning quickly on my heels, I made my way back to where my night had started, climbing silently into Tristian's window. Making my way back to where I had left him hours before, I laid my hands on him, whispering softly but urgently, trying to wake him.

Leaning down until my lips touched his ear, I insistently said his name, getting louder each time in my bid to wake him. So focused was I on this that I was unprepared when he turned his head and caught my lips with his, wrapping his arms around me to hold me in place. Frozen, I sat as his lips moved over mine, caught by surprise at the feeling. Jerking back from his lips, but still held in his arms, I watched as his sleepy eyes opened and realized it was me. I guess I expected shock and to be pushed from his arms, not the smile that curled his lips and the warm, sure press of his fingers on my back trying to pull me toward him. Moving my hands to his chest, I pushed back to separate us, seeing a frown mar his face before I took my eyes from his and he released me. With unsteady legs, I got up from the bed, keeping my face averted to hide the blush I could feel burning it. Remembering why I came back, I took a deep breath to calm my nerves and turned back to face him, taking a quick step back when I found him standing right behind me. Knowing I couldn't leave to avoid what just happened, I ignored it. I was probably making too much out of it, anyway—who knows who he thought I was?

Turning my gaze to his chin, I blurted out, "We need to wake your father," before he had a chance to speak. Turning on my heels, I went for the door. A hand shot past me, landing firmly on it and blocking my exit. Keeping my back to him, I said, "We need to wake your father, Tristian, now. It's a matter of life or death," I finished, waiting to see what he would do. With deliberate slowness, he removed his hand from the door, allowing me to release a breath I hadn't been aware that I was holding. Pulling the door open before he changed his mind, I made my way toward his father's room, stopping when a hand closed around my upper arm.

"Go into the sitting room, we'll join you in a moment," Tristian said, in a deep voice that sent a shiver through me. Obeying without question, I went and sat on the couch, silently waiting for them to join me. After about ten minutes they finally came.

"What's this about Misty?" A grumpy Crowley asked as he took the seat across from me, leaving Tristian to join me on the sofa. I really should have thought about the seating arrangements before taking my seat, I thought, before pushing that aside and getting down to what I came to tell him.

"I was out walking a few hours ago and noticed two strange men," I began, but was interrupted by Tristian.

"What the hell were you thinking of walking home this late by yourself? You should have woken me. Do you realize what could have happened to you?" he yelled.

Before he could go on, I cut in, "Will you shut up, now is not the time! Anyway, I saw two men and something didn't seem right, so I followed them. I ended up following them straight to the Elder Gillon's home. After he let them in, I snuck around to the back of the house and found a window to listen to them through. They were talking about you and the trouble you were giving them about the new lottery winners. The one suggested that they kill you now, but Gillon said that it would have to wait until after the council meeting, so no one got suspicious. He said he wasn't worried because he had the necessary votes"—stopping for a moment to collect my thoughts, I looked at Crowley and Tristian, who both wore the identical look of disbelief. Needing to finish the story, I said, "Then they started talking about one of the lottery winners being Gillon's replacement and how he was only supposed to have been assigned here for two years, not five. One of the men called him 'Jalic,' like that was his real name. Finally they asked him for a vid disc with his report. After some banging around, he gave it to them and left the room. The quiet one who hadn't spoken talked about killing him, but the other said that if it became an issue, his replacement would do it. After that, they left and I followed them again, I followed them right to the Loyalist cavern where the guards stood aside to allow them to enter."

"Did they see you?" Crowley demanded, fear lacing his voice.

Shaking my head, I said, "No, I was careful to stay in the shadows and far enough back that I wouldn't be noticed."

"I knew that there was something wrong, but I never imagined that Gillon wasn't one of us," Crowley whispered in shock.

"That's impossible. I remember Gillon from the time I was a child, he is one of us," I declared, waiting for him to deny it.

"Yes, Gillon is one of us or was one of us. This man 'Jalic' is an imposter made to look like Gillon and infiltrate us. The Gillon we knew is most likely dead. Killed after they tortured him for the information that he had," Crowley said, slamming his hand down in frustration. Rising from his chair, he paced the room like a caged animal before turning on us. "You two go back to bed. Misty, stay here the rest of the night. I don't want you being seen and recognized in case there are others out there." With that said, he turned and went to his office, closing the door behind him.

Left with Tristian, the silence in the room became awkward and I was about to disobey Crowley and just leave when I was stopped by the hand that grabbed mine. Tugging me from the couch, Tristian pulled me behind him to his room and straight to his bed. Laying down next to me, he wrapped his arms around me, pulling me tight until my back was flush with his chest. For the longest time, I waited for him to say something, but it never came. Eventually, I closed my eyes and let sleep claim me in the safety of his arms.

Chapter 6

Today is the day we leave this prison behind. Tensely, I wait in my kitchen for Tristian and Crowley to come to review our plans and help me tell the girls the truth. The silence in the kitchen is ominous as the girls and I eat our meager meal, their eyes skidding to me every few seconds as if they sense there is something wrong. Finishing the last of our meal, we work together to clean the kitchen before moving into the living room. Seeing that they were going to keep going to their room to escape my presence, I stopped them, telling them to sit. Quietly, we sat there for almost twenty minutes before our company came, no one saying a word. The knock on the door was a relief for the anxious girls, who both jumped and ran to answer it. Escorting Tristian and Crowley to me, they turned to leave, surprised when I told them to sit again, not expecting me to want them to stay. Getting up without another word, I went and collected Rose's gifts. When I reentered the room, everyone was seated and awaiting me.

Retaking my seat, I looked at the girls, dread coursing in my stomach for what I had to say. "I know that I haven't been myself since Rose's lottery. I am sorry if I have scared you, but I am sorrier for what I must now do,"

I began, hating myself as I looked into their sad, confused faces. "Rose showed me something the morning of the lottery that I am going to share with you. I know what I'm about show and tell you will be hard to accept, but you will have to be strong and face it. What I want you to do now is let me say what I'm about to and not interrupt." Taking a deep breath, I continued, "Today the two of you, Tristian, and I will be leaving this place and making our way to the surface."

"What are you talking about, we can't," Josie began, before being cut off by Crowley.

"Josie, Tina, I wish for you to remain silent until your sister is finished," he demanded, waiting until he had their stunned agreement before nodding at me to continue.

"What we can't do is remain here. On the day of Rose's murder"—and yes, it was murder, no matter what our government chose to call it—"she brought me these items." Laying them out on the table in front of them, I said, "She told me that I had to take the two of you and escape. This is a map of the caverns and this is a secret internal government video made when the first of our people were forced into these caves." Spreading the map in front of them, I continued, "We have been lied to, the caverns are more vast than anyone has ever suspected and filled with others like us, who were forced to serve monsters who destroyed the world above. The truth you find in this video will prove that they have lied to us in more ways than you can imagine, but know this right now––it is the truth and you must accept it. After you see this you will not be allowed to leave and hide, but must stay and hear our plans, so we can be free of this evil place." Waving my hand to Crowley and Tristian, I said, "They know what's on here and how hard it will be to see it, so they have come here to give you support." Dropping to my knees, I reached out and took their hands, squeezing them tightly. "Please, for the sake of your sanity, accept it, but do not dwell on what we cannot change," I whispered, before releasing them and turning on the vid display.

Blazing anger rushed through me as those hated voices began to speak. Using that anger, I focused, keeping my eyes glued to the girls I watched as the horror of the truth filled them. It was soul-crushing to watch all happiness and trust in the world fade from their eyes. Not allowing myself to be a coward and hide from what I told them to accept, I waited as the last words sounded and the twins raced to the bathroom, losing their dinner and innocence. After twenty minutes, they rejoined us, their ravaged faces telling the story, clinging to one another like babes. Walking to them slowly, I opened my arms, and as if that is what they were waiting for, they rushed to me, knocking us all to our knees. Holding them to me, I rocked the. I was the only mother they ever really knew, their protector. They expected me to keep the world safe for them. It broke my heart that I couldn't keep this from them, but forced them to see it and know that safety was just an illusion that could be taken at any time. As I held them, willing their pain from their bodies to mine, I swore that I wouldn't fail them again. My life meant nothing; if I had to give it, so be it. I would get them out of this place. They would live out their days in peace, unafraid of the passing of time and the consequences that it brought in this place.

Giving them one last squeeze, I helped them to the couch, which was a little hard since they refused to release each other. Squatting down so I could look them in the eye, I said, "We are leaving this place soon, so that"—I pointed to the discarded vid display on the table—"is not your fate. Your fate is to be among the first of us in thousands of years to walk upon the land above." I let none of the doubt I felt show. "Now you can tell no one about what you have learned; it will put everyone in danger. This must remain here."

A sniffling Tina found her voice at my words. "But what about my friends, what about Weston? I can't leave him behind—we tell each other everything. He has to know. We can bring him with us."

Shaking my head, I firmly told her, "No, we can't, I sorry," wanting to convey that there was no room for negotiation.

"That's not fair!" she wailed, pointing an accusing finger at Tristian. "Then why is he coming? Why can you bring him and I can't bring my boyfriend? I'll be alone if we don't take him. There are no boys up there."

"Enough!" I yelled. "Do you think I don't want to take him? Do you think I don't want to take everyone? We can't," I stated, through with discussing the subject. This is why I hadn't told them before now. Taking a calming breath, I said, "In a two hours, a meeting will take place. We will make our move then. Now listen as Crowley and Tristian walk you through the plan."

Taking my seat across from them, I tried to reign back my anger. Tina had always been the more self-absorbed of the twins, worried about how things would affect her, not those around her. One wrong move could see us killed, but instead of her first thoughts being for the safety of her family, they were for her boyfriend and her selfish needs. Turning my attention to the issue at hand, I listened as Crowley finished telling them the plan and what was expected of them. No sooner had the last word left his mouth then Tina jumped up and raced to her room.

Pulling my eyes from my retreating sister, I looked at an overwhelmed Josie. "You understand what we must do?"

"I understand, I'll go talk to her and pack," she whispered, with a dazed look in her eyes. She took the clothing that Tristian offered her and followed her sister's path. Knocking softly at the door, she whispered a few words, then entered her room to prepare for her new life.

Ignoring the sympathy in his eyes, I asked Crowley, "You've made a copy of the map, but what about the vid disc—should you take it or should I leave it hidden here?"

Thinking about it for a moment before answering, he said, "Leave it here. After it's noticed that you're gone, the house will be searched, but your hiding place will be overlooked. Especially with the blood we are leaving planted here. It will be assumed you were killed. We already know that I'm under suspicion and leaving it with another Elder would be just as bad."

Agreeing that was the safest bet, I looked to the clock and realized that it was almost time. Picking up my pile of clothing, I murmured that I would be back. Stopping at the girls' room as I went, I told them to get dressed through the locked door before going to my room to do the same, wanting to give Tristian and his father a private moment to say good-bye.

A kind of numb calm had descended over me as I prepared myself for what I must do. By the time I was finished putting on the brightly colored clothing and walked to the mirror to see the results, I was ready. Ready to do anything that I had to do to make sure Rose's sacrifice wasn't in vain, my sisters would survive. Gathering up the rest of what was needed into the bag, I took one final look around my room before throwing the cloak over my shoulders that would hide my disguise and joined the others, who were already waiting on me in the living room. The girls stared at the floor, nervously shifting from one foot to the other, not raising their heads to look at me even though they knew I was there, the stiffening of their bodies betraying them.

Ignoring them, I went directly to Crowley, stopping a few steps from him. Intense grief shifted through me at the thought of saying good-bye to him. He had been the closest thing I had to a father through the years. He was always watching out for me, never getting angry, no matter how many times I asked him something. For all his faults, he was a good man who served his people, never expecting anything in return and always ready to do what was needed. He was a man who knew death stalked him, but instead of saving himself, he stayed for the same reason I was leaving because we were needed to lead our people to freedom. Seeing my conflict, he stepped forward and pulled me into his arms saying with his embrace what I couldn't form into words.

"You can do this, you are a survivor. You will lead them into the light and I will not stop until all our people can follow and join you," he whispered, squeezing me tightly before stepping back. Blinking back my tears, I nodded, my head and my throat too tight to allow words to escape.

Watching as he went to my sisters and embraced them, I felt as if the world was shattering around me, but it was when he embraced Tristian—I felt the world become destroyed. A hard look graced Tristian's face as he released his father as if he had bury all softness deep, where it could never be touched again. Closing my eyes, I felt his pain that he refused to show and I knew it well. It was the same pain I had felt when Rose had said that she wasn't coming with us. Though Tristian's pain was much worst. At least a portion of my family would join me in the new world, but his would remain behind. I silently vowed that he would understand one day that all his family had not been left behind. That my sisters and I would not become a replacement family, but an extension of the one that he already had. Stepping forward to stand next to Tristian, I saw the grateful look in his father's eyes at my action. He had nothing to be grateful for—Tristian was my friend and for good or evil I stood by those I loved and would protect them with a fierceness the likes of which even the government could not stop.

Without another word or glance back, Crowley left, leaving a void in his wake. No one spoke as we listened to the tick of the clock counting the time. As the chimes of the clock rung out, it was time to go. The factories had let out and the streets would be packed, so no one would notice our movements, we would just be faces in the crowd. Gathering together, we made our way out with Tristian leading the way and me bringing up the rear, the girls safely between us. It took us twenty minutes to reach the alley near the cavern entrance that we had to hide in. Tensely, we waited as soldiers lounged near its entrance, until finally what we were waiting for happened. Alarms sounded—a large brawl was happening one street over, our distraction.

Between this and the meeting of the Elders, the soldiers would be stretched thin. We wouldn't get a better chance. Making sure that the soldiers that had just left their posts were really gone, Tristian and I each grabbed one of the girls' arms and ran. Terror gave me speed, pulling a slow Tina behind me who kept looking over her shoulder. Finally reaching the small door next to the large metal gates of the cavern, we pushed it open, rushing inside. Total blackness engulfed us as our labored breath echoed in the darkness. I could hear Tristian as he fumbled with his bag, searching for a light. The girls had just started to whimper when a light began to glow from his hand. The small light made no dent in the darkness, just allowed us to see one another's terrified faces. Keeping a hand on Tina, I groped through the air until I found Josie's, causing her to jump.

Dragging them behind me, I moved forward until I was flush with Tristian. Nudging my chin straight ahead, he turned to see what I saw. A sliver of light so thin you would think you imagined it winked at us from the distance. Nodding that he understood, he turned to the girls, raising his finger to his lips for silence before turning toward the phantom light and beginning our journey through the Cavern of Death. Fear is a living thing; I know because if I had gave myself to it, it would have strangled me. Focusing on the light that grew as we journeyed farther in, I blocked everything else from my mind, tightening my grips on the girls to silence the sounds they were making. I don't know how long it took to reach the source of the light, but in inky blackness it had seemed like hours. Every step we took I expected a hand to reach out and pull me in, trapping me in this wretched place. Relief coursed through me when I saw the light was coming from under a door, there was a way out, and we wouldn't be trapped here wandering aimlessly in the dark forever.

As Tristian opened the well-oiled door, light rushed in, blinding us. Quickly, he closed it, partially to give our eyes time to adjust and to hide us from passing eyes. Waiting until he received nods from everyone, he pulled it open enough to check for people. Seeing no one, he motioned for us to follow. Keeping the girls behind me, we joined him on the grated walkway the door opened to. Machines and vats filled the huge space, but that wasn't what caught and held our gazes. What held our horrified gazes were the bodies hanging on hooks high in the air, level to us, swinging in the air from the large fans that blew on them before being released into the bin below.

The moans ripped my attention away from the scene in front of me. Leaping toward their retreating forms, I grabbed Josie, covering her mouth with my hand, Tristian doing the same with Tina as they wildly fought us. Terrified of being heard, I brought my lips as close to her ear as I could and whispered, "Is that how you want to die up on that hook? If they hear so much as a small whimper that will be your fate." Harsh, I know, but now wasn't the time to comfort her. Only strength would see us through this. After a few moments, my words seemed to sink in as she stopped struggling. Looking into her eyes, I waited to see what I needed before releasing her. I removed my hand slowly to make sure that she was under control. Satisfied, I went to help Tristian who was trying to hold Tina down, saying the same to her that I told Josie. I watched as her need for self-preservation kicked in and she went completely still.

The sound of approaching footsteps froze us in place, breaking the trance. We dove back into the darkness that we just came from. Holding my hands over the girl's mouths, not daring to breath, we waited to be discovered. Tristian, a knife tight in his grip, crouched at the side of the door ready to attack if they entered the room. After a tense moment, the footsteps passed us and faded into the distance, causing a shudder to pass through my body in relief. Quietly, we waited, letting as much time as we dared pass before venturing back onto the walkway. Keeping our eyes averted from the bodies, we moved with as much speed as we dared, searching for the entrance into the Loyalist cavern.

We had almost lost Tina twice because she kept stopping and looking behind her. Annoyed, I pushed her in front of me and kept her there. Behind vats and walls, we hid whenever we heard so much as a creek, terrified of being discovered, until finally we saw what we were searching for. High up in the air, accessed by a walkway, was the door we needed. Two workers in white coats lounged by the stairs that we needed to take. Looking around for a distraction, I grabbed a small metal object near me and threw it. It worked—when they heard the sound they went running and so did we. Dashing up the stairs to the door, we skidded to a halt before opening it. Opening the door a crack, we listened for sound, and not hearing anything we took a chance and opened it enough for Tristian to peek his head out. Shooting out his hand, he waved it for us to follow and I got my first view of the Loyalist Cavern.

Chapter 7

It wasn't what I expected—while it was infinitely better than our homes, it appeared run-down, abandoned. Ignoring the thought, I kept a sharp gaze out for anyone as we quickly removed our cloaks, keeping them over our arms to hide our bags. Moving at a quick pace, we headed for a group of buildings about five hundred feet away. Getting there, we dodged deep into an alley and huddled together as we tried to catch our breath and listen for sounds of pursuit. As we listened and heard no cry of alarm, my mind began to turn to something else I wasn't hearing, people. The harder I listened, the less I heard—no footsteps, no buzz of electricity from the homes, nothing. Easing back from the group, I softly made my way down the alley until I reached the back of the house. A slightly open glass door caught my attention. Quietly, I made my way to it, my eyes darting to the other houses looking for signs for life. Carefully I eased the door open and looked within, freezing at what I saw.

The hand that came around and covered my mouth caused me to jump in surprise. Relaxing into Tristian so he would know I knew it was him, he released me. Indicating for him to grab the girls, I started forward only getting to raise my foot before his arm shot out to stop me. Turning to see his face I mouthed "Trust me" and a second later he released me, going around the corner to grab the girls. Moving forward, I walked into the bare room, not a piece of furniture present. A stale smell filled the air as if it had been vacant for a very long time.

Hearing them enter behind me, I asked, "What do you think Tristian?" wanting to know if he felt it, too.

"I don't know, but something isn't right. It's as if the area has been abandoned," he said, moving to look through the door to the rest of the house.

Yes, but why was it abandoned? That's the question. Placing my bag on the floor, I motioned for the girls to sit. "Stay there, don't explore, don't speak above a whisper, and stay away from the windows," I told them as I sat down and pulled out the map.

Sitting down next to me and studying the map, Tristian said, "We have to figure out how far we're inside the entrance—it's the only way we'll be able to find the fissure."

"What do you mean we have to find the fissure? I thought we were going through the shaft, the easy way," Tina interrupted.

Not bothering to look up, I said, "Do you see anyone in this home? Anyone in the streets? Do you hear the sounds of people? No, you don't, which means there is no one for us to blend in with. If we tried to go through to another cave, they'd know we don't belong," I finished, unable to keep the exasperation out of my voice at her density in the situation.

"That doesn't mean anything. We have to go to the next cavern," she argued, making no sense.

Raising my eyes from the map to look at her, I asked, "Why do we have to go to the next cavern, Tina?" wondering why it mattered to her.

Turning her head to look out the window, she stuttered, "It's just that Josie and I can't climb as well as you two," her face flushing.

"I it will be OK. Tristian and I will be there to help you two, there's nothing to worry about," I explained, hoping that this would allay her fears.

But instead of acknowledging my words, her face turned stubborn and her lips into a thin line.

Shaking my head, I gave my attention to Tristian. "We have to get moving, we can't risk someone realizing we're missing. I think the entrance to our cave is in this direction, but I'm not sure how far we are into the Loyalist Cavern. Let's move in this direction and see if we can get a better sense of the distance."

Slowly nodding his head, he countered, "I think you're right, that's the best plan of action, but I think we should go farther over to this side, where the fissure is located. That way we're close enough to access it quickly, especially if we're seen."

"It sounds like a plan," I agreed, wanting to get as far from here as we could. There was something very wrong about this place and I had a bad feeling.

Putting the map back in my bag, I motioned for the girls to rise as Tristian went to check the way before we left, and after a moment he signaled for us to follow. Keeping the girls between us, we made our way through the twists and turns of the houses, never hearing a sound until about four hours later. We had stopped at another abandoned house to check the map, going to the top floor to get a better view. We could see the entrance to our cavern in the distance, the fissure was closer to it than we realized. Wanting to give the girls a rest before moving on was the only thing that kept us from getting caught.

We had been just about to put the water away when we heard the voices. "I don't understand why we have to patrol the streets. There's no way they'd be this far toward us. They're headed in the other direction," the voice whined.

"The informer said that there was an exit in this cavern. Once they realized they couldn't hide among the population here, they would make for it," the answering voice growled.

"That impossible, we'd know if there was a way to the surface through here," the first voice scoffed.

"It's an unexplored exit on an old map, who knows where it really leads to, but the informer told the commander that the girl said it was there. So we will search until they are found," the second voice said, fading as it moved past us down the street.

Who could have told them? We had been so careful of everything, only the three of us had known, and Crowley would have died rather than betray us. As I looked around at the others, it was Tina my gaze caught and held. The look on her face before she could hide it told me everything—it was the look of guilt. There were only three of us who had known up until two hours before our departure. Focusing more sharply on Tina, I wondered why had she kept stopping. Why was she looking behind her as if she was waiting for someone? "Why" I whispered, knowing that it was her, but needing to hear her say it.

"I don't know what you're talking about," she answered, with defiance in her voice.

I think it was her defiant tone that made me snap. She used it whenever she had been caught in a lie. I couldn't help what I did next; maybe if she had been apologetic or fearful I could had controlled myself, but to see her defiantly siting there as if she hadn't just murdered someone. It was too much. I had never laid a hand on her before, no matter what she had done, so she was unprepared when I launched myself across the room and backhanded her before pinning her to the ground and wrapping me hands around her throat.

I truly think I would have killed her if Tristian hadn't been there. Josie had grabbed my arm, trying to pull it from Tina's neck, but she didn't have the strength to battle the strength my anger gave me. It wasn't an insane anger, but a controlled one. As I stared into Tina's eyes, I saw absolute terror as she realized she had pushed me too far, family or no family. She clawed at my hands in desperation, scoring deep marks that I ignored, using the focus on my task so completely that I was able to block all feelings, pain, love—I felt none of it.

Another moment and I think she would have been dead if not for Tristian. Grabbing me, he pulled me from her body, taking me to the other side of the room. I didn't fight him or struggle, but just watched her with disinterest as she gasped for breath. Josie rushed to her side, gathering her now weeping form into her arms as she gazed at me with fear and guilt. Had she known what Tina had done? Of course she had, they share the same room. She had rushed to the room after Tina to calm her. Was Tina still there when she got there or already gone? Did it matter either way? She hadn't warned us and was just as guilty as Tina. Just as much a traitor, but I needed her to say it. "Do you foolish children realize what you have done?" I calmly asked. From the expressions on their faces, the quietness of my voice terrified them more than screams would have. Not waiting for them to answer, I told them, "Do you realize that you have murdered Crowley. That you have murdered Tristian's father." Seeing that they were about to deny it, I continued before they could speak. "Yes, you have, as sure as if you had stabbed him through the heart, you have killed him. The two of you have most likely killed the whole cavern if he cannot convince the soldiers and government that no one else knows about the truth about the Cavern of Death," I asserted, as they shook their heads in horror, wanting to deny my words.

"Enough, Misty," Tristian interrupted.

Turning in his arms to look at him, I saw the pain in his face that no words could comfort before a hardness came over his face. Acknowledging his request with my eyes, I rose from his arms and went to the side of the window, needing to check if we had been heard. When I was sure that there was no one about, I stepped back from the sight of the widow and looked down at my sisters. My hand prints stood out sharply against Tina's pale skin, almost looking like a necklace with the complete circle they formed. Tears fell down both their faces as they huddled together and silently cried. Walking over to them, I knelt down until I was even with them. "Stop your tears now and pull yourselves together. Both of you look at me now," I ordered, having no sympathy for their pain. "We have to leave soon or we will be as good as dead." Moving to stand, I was stopped by Josie's words.

"You're still taking us with you?" she timidly asked, always having more courage than Tina. It was her quietness that made people believe that she was the weaker sister.

"What's been done cannot be undone. Rose gave her life to make sure that you would have one. She unselfishly gave her life for her family and no matter how angry I am at you, you are my family and I can give no less than she has," I explained, as if dealing with infants who had not yet learned about honor or family loyalty. Taking a deep breath, I hardened my voice so that they would understand what I said next I meant with everything in me. "But should you ever betray us again, I will slit your throats without a thought. Family or no family, I will protect Tristian—I owe his father this. I owe his father his son's life for the sacrifice that he was forced to make because of you two." Standing without another word, I went to collect my things.

I could hear the shuffling behind me as they gathered their things, their sniffling stopped at my words. "Do you have an idea where the fissure is now?" I asked Tristian.

"Yes, I have a general idea. If we keep moving south we should find the entrance," he replied, before turning to Tina. "What exactly did you tell Weston about the fissure?" he asked in a bland voice.

"I only told him that there was a spot that may lead to the surface in this cavern, but we weren't going to take it unless we had to because you weren't sure where it lead to or if it was clear. I told him to meet us at the Cavern of Death so we could travel together because we were going to head into the next cavern past the Loyalist Cavern," she hoarsely answered.

"So they'll be searching the whole city, that's good. We'll have a better chance if they're not concentrated in one area," he concluded, picking up his pack.

"Tristian I'm…" Tina began.

"As your sister said, what's done is done. Let's not speak of it again," Tristian tersely said, cutting her off and moving to the door.

Waving the girls in front of me, I brought up the rear as we made our way out of our hiding place and cautiously back into the street. At least we knew that they were looking for us—this way we could be more vigilant. Making our way quietly south, we dodged two patrols easily, hearing them long before we saw them. By the time we had finally made our way to the south wall, we were all exhausted, physically and mentally. Finding a defendable house ,Tristian lead us in to rest and eat while he pulled out the map to see if there was anything on it he had missed that could tell him where our exit was hiding.

Leaving them in the room, I made my way to the house's kitchen and checked to see if there was still water. Turning the handle on the sink, I smiled when water started to pour from it. Leaving it to run, I searched the room looking for anything that we might use to carry extra water. Hitting the jackpot, I found two jugs with lids and quickly filled them before cupping my hands and drinking my fill. Taking the two jugs back to our little hideaway, I went around and collected everyone's water containers, urging them to drink them dry before taking them to get refiled. Bringing the girls their water, I whispered for them to "close their eyes and rest" before finding a wall and doing the same. Whispering to Tristian to "wake me in twenty minutes" so he could rest while I stood guard, I closed my eyes for a quick nap.

Fear shot through me when I opened my eyes, a hand covering my mouth. Seeing Tristian's face in front of mine, I calmed enough to hold in my scream. Voices could be heard clearly outside the house. Nodding to the girls, we made our way to them, placing our hands above their mouths before waking them. Terror shot through their eyes when they opened them and stayed there when they heard the crude laughs coming from outside. When we were sure they wouldn't scream, we removed our hands, motioning for them to be silent. Crawling toward the window to hear them better, I sat very still and listened.

"Yes, sir, I understand."

"Well, what did the commander say?"

"They still haven't found the escape Contributors, we're to begin a house-to-house search to make sure they aren't hiding in one. They're going to send out perimeter teams to all the cave walls to find this fissure and make sure that they don't escape through there."

"Are you kidding? We're to check all these houses? It'll take weeks!"

"Stop complaining, more teams are coming. Let's move to the beginning of the block and work our way down in rows so we don't miss any."

"Sounds best. Is there a reward for whoever catches them?"

"Don't worry, Paul, I'm sure we'll be allowed to play with them before we kill them." The soldier said, him and his friend laughing and making suggestions on how they were going to play with us as they moved away.

Jumping up, we all moved quickly, gathering our things and leaving the house. Moving faster than before, we ran silently after Tristian, stopping and moving at his signal. We could hear voices approaching in the distance, we were so focused on them we didn't notice the silent threat until we were standing in front of it. We had turned to take an alley, quickly moving through, and we didn't hear the two soldiers that stepped in from the other side. I don't know who was more shocked, them or us, but luckily we recovered first. Turning on our heels, we dashed back the way we came, their shouts and heavy steps following us.

We ran. We ran until we thought our hearts would burst and kept going. The sound of more soldiers approaching gave us strength. In and out of allies we dashed as they got closer and closer. Soon they would have us and our deaths would not be quick or easy. It was by sheer luck that we found what we had been searching for. Forced down an alley where the houses butted the cavern wall, we were trapped. Making our way to the back, thinking that this was it, I took out my knife, ready to kill my sisters rather than let the soldiers have them. Luck or fate was on our side, as we reached the very back of the alley and saw it, the fissure. Relief and fear coursed through me as I pushed the girls forward and yelled at them to run. Turning sideways, they squeezed into the crack one after the other until I was the only one left. I could see the soldiers at the head of the alley waving to others, and not waiting to see what they were doing, I followed the others into the darkness.

It was a tight squeeze for the first sixty to seventy feet as we pushed and pulled each other through. It widened up after that, enough so that we could move side by side. In the distance we could hear the voices of the soldiers. I didn't think they were pursing yet, but it was only a matter of time, most likely they were waiting for equipment to follow us with. Taking time we didn't have, we stopped long enough to strip off our outer layer of clothing, stuffing them in our bags. Our less baggy climbing clothes would make it easier and safer to move through the cavern.

Silently and as quickly as we dared, we moved through the pitch blackness with only little lights to guide our way. Every step we took was dangerous at our speed, unable to check for cracks or chasms in the floor. Hours passed and still we heard no pursuers, but we didn't lessen our pace, falling and tumbling on each other as we tripped over unseen rocks. The girls, unused to the physical strain, were unable to get back up after the last fall. Completely exhausted, they tried, but their legs were unable to hold them. Looking to Tristian, I saw the resignation in his eyes as he took out food and water and announced that "it was safe enough that we would rest here for a moment."

After seeing to the girl's needs, I collapsed next to Tristian, leaning into his side. Closing my eyes, I allowed my head to fall back to the wall. It was only a matter of time before they came after us. Professional cave climbers that wouldn't hide their light like we do, but allow it to shine bright, uncaring if we saw it. This would allow them to move much faster than us. Opening my eyes to our dim light, I looked to the girls, who valiantly held back their tears and I was proud of them. For all their mistakes, they hadn't gave a word of complaint at our pace, never faltering till now.

Moving my hand out slowly, I found what I was searching for and entwined my fingers with Tristian's, leaning my head onto his shoulder. I heard the sound as I sat there in the silence—it was faint and in the distance, but it was there; our reprieve was over. Tristian tensed next to me, tightening his hand and letting me know he had heard it, too. I squeezed my eyes shut before I pulled my weary body up and went to the girls.

Leaning down, I shook their shoulders. "We have to go," I whispered. I watched as they weakly opened their eyes and nodded that they understood. With sadness I stood back as they helped each other struggle to their feet, not making a sound of complaint. Wanting to slow our pace, but knowing we couldn't, I kept my words to myself as we moved forward.

They had found us. We had been slowed down by climbing, deep chasms, and wrong turns so much that they had caught up with us easily. Now we worked our way through a tunnel that I knew was going to be our death. Every sound that we made caused bits of rock to rain down upon us. The whole place was a cave-in waiting to happen and we were trapped within. Moving as fast as we could only brought us to the end sooner, literally. Reaching a large opening at the end of the tunnel, we stood there staring at our doom. There was no way out, we were trapped. A large ledge stood prominently high into the air, and going forward, Tristian began to climb, moving studiedly up. Hurrying to reach the top so he could throw down a rope to pull the girls up with, he wasn't quick enough. He had just finished pulling himself over the lip when the soldiers burst through. Turning to put myself in front of the girls, I was horrified to realize that they weren't next to me but near the soldiers.

Terrified, they tried to run to me, but it was too late. Their first step hadn't landed before hands wrapped into their hair, pulling them back, throwing them to the ground. Their screams shook the cavern as they clawed desperately at their captors' hands. I knew what was coming and I welcomed it—at least I knew that we would take our pursuers with us. At first dust rained down on us before small pebbles joined in. A rumbling began to sound as their screams of terror grew, a loud cracking sound our only warning before a large chuck of the ceiling came down near me, causing me to dive to the side or be crushed. In terror, the soldiers covered the girls' mouths, pulling them back into the tunnel, trying to escape. In a desperate move, I got to my feet and raced after them, but I was too late. The last look I had of my sisters was of them being dragged backward, silently pleading with me to save them.

I had almost reached them when the ceiling collapsed in front of our only exit, throwing me back with force. As I laid upon the ground, my last thought before the darkness took me was that I failed them and this tomb was my punishment for my failure.

Chapter 8

I woke with my head in Tristian's lap. Opening my eyes hurt, but what hurt more was the pain that tore through my heart, leaving an empty hole that my sisters once existed in. Burying it deep, I slowly rose with his help, fighting back tears that begged for freedom. The silence after a cave-in is eerie, and the sound of our breathing echoed in the silent space. Looking around, I fought not to let my fear take me, but we were trapped. Rocks that we could never move were piled in front of the tunnel, keeping me from my sisters, most likely trapped on the other side. Had they died quickly, crushed by the rocks, or where they buried deep, slowly suffocating, waiting for me to save them?

I couldn't hold back the sob that broke my throat at the thought of them hurt, alone, afraid, needing me. Pulling me into his chest, Tristian didn't try to quiet me or give me empty platitudes, but let me ride out my grief, absorbing it into him. When I was finally able to stop my body's racking sobs and fight them back into whimpering gasps, I was exhausted. I hurt both physically and mentally as the pain of my fall began to fill my grief-stricken mind.

Pressing firmly into Tristian, I wrapped myself around him, letting oblivion slowly claim me.

I don't know how long I slept, time had no meaning in the darkness. Blinking slowly, I sat there stiffly, waiting for my eyes to adjust. For a moment I panicked, thinking I was trapped here alone, that I had imagined Tristian's arms around me, until I realized his coat cushioned my head. Rising up slowly, the pain in my head still there, though fainter then before, I sat very still, listening for sound. It took a few moments, but finally found what I was looking for, there up on the ledge, a tiny sound broke the silence. Squinting my eyes, I saw a slight difference in the darkness, as if a tiny light was fighting to be seen.

Reaching my hand out, I found what I searched for and pulled my bag toward me. Groping around, I found the light and took it out. It blinded me for a moment, but after my eyes adjusting I got out the water and food, using it sparingly. I don't know why; it would just prolong our deaths. Putting back my meager supplies, the girls' packs caught my eye, causing me to fight back my grief. Pushing it aside, I pulled my aching body to its feet, ignoring the pain, and made my way to the ledge. Seeing the rope that Tristian had dropped, I wrapped my grip firmly around it and slowly pulled myself up. Hand over hand, I concentrated on reaching the top, my light clenched firmly between my teeth. Reaching the lip, I was met by Tristian who pulled me over, helping me to my feet.

Gripping my hand, he pulled me toward the wall, stopping a few feet away. "How are you feeling?" he asked.

"I'll be fine. Nothing's broken," I replied, looking around to see what he saw. He wouldn't have taken me to this spot if there wasn't something. It took a few moments to see what he saw or more precisely feel what he felt—a breeze. Moving forward, I held out my hand, looking for the source, and there—that was it! It was coming from a crack in the wall, not big enough to enter, with the stones that filled it. They weren't large like the ones that covered the entrance, but small enough to move if we were careful.

"I going to go down and get the packs, I want you to slowly start shifting this section here," Tristian said, before turning and leaving without another word.

Focusing on the job he had given me, I didn't hear him return and was startled when he got down next to me and started to work. We worked like this for days in silence, barely a word passing our lips, before we would fall exhaustedly asleep just to start again the next time we woke. It's hard to tell how much time had passed before it was cleared—enough for us to move through time having no meaning in this place. The day after we cleared it enough that we could have moved through, he wouldn't let us go, insisting that we rest first and collect our strength before going in because he didn't know what we would find.

As much as I wanted to rush in, I knew he was right. We ate much more than we had previously, wanting our strength before crawling into each other's arms to share our body heat, the cold of the cave more bearable this way. When we woke, our bodies were stiff from the cold and the hardness of the ground, and taking a few moments for ourselves, we moved in different directions for privacy.

During our quick breakfast, Tristian broke the silence. "We'll tie the rope to us, hooking us together. This way if there is a problem the other will be able to help."

"Agreed," I whispered, walking over to the edge and pulling the rope up. When I turned back, I saw that Tristian had already put our supplies away. Tying one end of the rope around me, he then tied the other end around his waist. Taking my pack from his hand—we had already emptied the girls' packs into ours to make it easier to carry—we moved into our hole, pushing our bags in front of us to make it easier to move through the small opening.

It was the right move. The farther we moved in, the tighter it became, making it hard to move, but it would have been impossible if the bags had been on our backs. Slowly and steadily we made our way forward, stopping every so often to widen the narrow space, the small movements causing our muscles to cramp. We were forced to sleep the first night in our little tunnel that seemed to have no end. Hour after hour we moved forward, turns and twists, up and down we went, until we final reached what I feared didn't exist: an exit. An exit that would have been Tristian's death if we hadn't been attached by the rope. One minute we were going forward, the next I was being dragged forward as Tristian free-fell into the darkness. If the tunnel had been any wider, we would have both fallen to our deaths. The narrowness saved us as I was able to wedge myself in, stopping our forward motion.

Gasping from the pain of the rope around my waist, I said, "Tristian are you OK?"

When he whispered "yes" I almost cried in relief. "There's a drop here, watch your step," he said drily, causing me to giggle. "Hold on, I'm going to see how deep it is," he ordered, making me wonder if he was losing it. Hold on? What else did he expect me to do? After a few moments of waiting, he said, "It's not too deep, are you secure enough that I can swing to the wall?"

Bracing my back and knees more firmly into the walls, I said, "I'm ready, go for it."

It took three swings for him to get a good grip. Each swing tore into my hands and body as I held him into the air.

"Misty, you OK?"

"Yeah, I'm good," I hoarsely answered, unable to keep the pain from my voice.

"I have a good hold, I want you to move slowly forward, keeping a tight hold on your pack. Mine fell to the ground, so it will be no help to us. We're going to need the climbing equipment in yours, so whatever you do, don't drop it. I'm on a small ledge, so if you fall I'll be able to hold us, but do me a favor and try not to test the theory."

Sarcastic bastard. Rolling my eyes, I un-wedged myself and inched forward, keeping a death grip on my bag. Reaching the edge, I put my light in my mouth and looked over. It was a sheer drop from here, no wonder he had gone flying—there was nothing to latch on to. Our exit jutted out and where I needed to be was about five feet under me. Wiggling my way back in, I got out a spike, hammer, and rope. Tying the rope to a clip and hooking it to the spike, I turned onto my back and went back to the edge, leaning out and hammering it into the solid rock before moving back and repacking my bag. Taking a deep breath, I went back onto my back and made my way out until I was in a sitting position with my legs in our tunnel and my upper body held by my grip on the rope that was hooked to the hoop on my harness.

Swinging my bag around, I put it on my back to free up my hands, then, taking a deep breath, I pulled myself out until I was dangling in the nothingness before repelling myself down to Tristian. Having more than enough climbing gear for both of us, since I had one of the girls', we easily made our way down to the cave's floor. The cave had a damp smell to it and also another that I couldn't place, an ammonia-type smell. Though weak, it was still powerful and grew more so the deeper we went in. Covering our noses and mouths with pieces of cloth to dampen the smell, we moved forward, the cave floor turning mushy. A strange sound echoed above us, and turning our light up, beady eyes stared back. I don't know if it was the light or our presence that disturbed them, but suddenly the little monsters took flight, swooping around us. Grabbing my arm, Tristian dragged me to a shelf of jutted rocks that we were able to hide under. In awe, we watched the black mass swoop and turn, having never seen anything the likes of it before except in school. Yes, that's where I knew these creatures from—they were supposed to be extinct, along with all other creatures. They were called bats, it was a night creature that hunted in the dark and once lived in caves. Amazed, I watched as they just disappeared down a small tunnel straight across from us.

"Come on, let's go before they come back," Tristian said, trying to pull me back the way we came.

Digging my heels in, I shook my head and pointed at the way the bats went. "No, we have to go that way, it's the way out!" I excitedly said.

"Are you crazy, if those things come back through, we'll have no place to hide and besides, we don't know where that leads to."

Ripping my arm from his grip, I ran for the tunnel. "No, I remember this from school. These animals are night creatures and hunt outdoor—they'd have an exit and that's it!" Climbing into the tunnel, I looked behind me at the stubborn man. "I've trusted you. Now it's your turn to trust me," I declared before moving in, sure that he would follow.

"You couldn't find an exit that smelled better?" he complained from behind me.

Smiling, I rushed forward, not wanting to be caught in here if the bats returned any more than he did. For all of my jumping in and saying that it was an exit, I was only guessing and I hoped I was right because those things freaked me out and I didn't want to be trapped in this small space with them. After about fifteen minutes, I started to worry until I smelled something. Excited, I moved quicker, ignoring Tristian's warnings to slow down. A pale light in the darkness loomed ahead of me. Reaching it, I put my hand down and came up with nothing. Off balance, my body fell forward, my chest hitting the ground as I stared at the abyss that I almost pitched myself into. Scrambling back until my hand were safely on a firm surface, my heart beating in fear, I almost broke down and cried thinking that again we had only found a dead end, until I looked up and saw something that I had never expected to see in my life, the sky. It was far up in the distance, but it was there. "Tristian," I dazedly said, trying to form words.

"What's wrong?" he whispered urgently, scared by my voice. I could feel him gripping my leg, shaking it, trying to get me to speak but for a long moment. I couldn't, unable to put my thoughts to words. "Damn you, answer me now!" Tristian demanded, yelling, uncaring of who heard him, too afraid of my silence to let it continue.

"I see it, Tristian. I see the sky," I whispered in awe.

For a long time we sat in silence as he digested what I said. Most likely he was as overwhelmed as I was. "How do we reach it, Misty?" he finally asked, breaking me from my daze.

Yes, I wanted to reach it, feel it upon my skin. "There's a narrow ravine here that we can fit into. We had better use the spikes to get out of this tunnel, because it looks like a long drop if we misstep, but after that we'll be able to easily climb up." Wiggling my fingers toward him, I said, "I'll need your spikes and hammer. I never took my bag off my back, so I can't reach mine."

After a few seconds, I felt the tools graze my fingers, and I greedily grasped them and pulled them forward. With shaking hands, I reached out, leaning into the abyss while Tristian held my feet, wanting to get some hooks down low as well as high so that we had hand and foot holds. It seemed to take forever to get everything done before I could tell Tristian to pull me back. Sliding the hammer back to him, I waited impatiently for him to get his supplies back into the bag.

When he finally said that he was ready, I was about to jump out of my skin with my excitement. With slow, even movements, I went forward, grasping the spike in front of me as I twisted and turned my way out. Finally free, I could reach both sides of the wall easily, which would make this an easy climb. The first that we have had since we began our journey. Moving to get out of Tristian's way, I waited until he was all the way out and securely situated before I started my journey up. The smells that began to assault my senses were overwhelming. I had never smelled anything like them before, and had nothing to compare them to. The pale light of the moon grew brighter the closer we got, acting like shards of glass through my eyes after being so long in the darkness. As I reached up and felt the lip of the small ravine, my hand landed on something soft and wet, causing me to jerk back. Not about to be a coward when I was so close, I forced myself to put my hand back and pull myself the rest of the way to freedom.

Dragging myself out of the hole across from the sweet-smelling green stuff that surrounded me, I stared at in wonder until I came to my senses and scrambled out of Tristian's way. I can honestly say that I will remember my first look at the surface of our world to the day I die. Looking around, it was a vast open space unlike anything I had ever seen in my life and it was as terrifying as it was exhilarating. Where we came out was slightly high in the air, high enough that I could see the tops of trees. Even in the dark I could see that they were green in color, the moon shining as bright as day would have been in the cavern. Bright stars glowed in the sky above and large mountains in the distance. Bringing my face to look at the ground, I started to shake, the openness of this world making me nervous. A pretty pink thing caught my eye and with shaking hands, I reached forward to touch the softest thing I had ever felt before, the petal of a flower. Leaning forward, I brought my nose to it and smelled the most amazing thing. Though I knew the names of most of these things, their smells, their feel, and even most of their uses were never explained to us, but two of those things could never have been explained. Now that I'd seen them in life, only experience allowed me to understand.

Like a child, I was giddy in my excitement. I pulled my shoes and socks from my feet, wanting to feel the grass bare against them. It tickled at first, but I set them firmly down, kneading my toes into the grass. It was amazing. With a huge smile, I turned to Tristian. Who was in the same state as I was, overwhelmed with everything he was seeing.

Standing up, I walked cautiously, the light breeze tickling me with warm air. A splashing sound caught my attention and wanting to go explore, I ran over to Tristian, grabbing his hand and pulling him to his feet. Tugging him behind me, we cautiously went toward the sound that was not far from us. It was a large body of water and it flowed through the land. Moving closer, I noticed that is was surrounded by animals, the most amazing things I had ever seen. They showed no fear of us, just raised their heads to stare as if they were as curious of us as we were of them.

Not wanting to frighten them, I slowly lowered myself to the ground. Smiling, I lifted my face to gaze up at Tristian. "Well, Tristian, I guess your father was right," I whispered.

Lowering down next to me, he curiously asked, "My father was often right about many things, but which are you referring to?"

"I asked him if he thought the world above still existed and do you what he told me."

Tristian shook his head.

"That he believed the land would heal itself and life would find a way to rebuild from the destruction we had caused." Looking out at the beauty in front of us, I continued, "and one day our people would walk upon it once more."

"And we have to find a way to free our people, so that they can join us," he finished for me. Moving closer to him, I laid my head against his chest as he leaned against the tree behind him, wrapping his arms around me. Together we sat like that until sleep took us, enjoying the magic and peace of our new world.

Chapter 9

Strange sounds surrounded me, and opening my eyes to see what it was, I was blinded by pain as if shards of glass were being gouged into my eyes. Crying out, I threw myself from Tristian, curling onto my knees. I wrapped my head with my arms, hiding my eyes from the source of my pain. My cries must have woken Tristian, because his curses soon joined my cries. Ripping at my outer shirt, I pulled it off, keeping my eyes squeezed shut as I ripped it into strips and wrapped it around my head. Slowly, I tested it, barely opening my eyes, adding a second strip before it muted the light, enough to stop the pain, but I could see. Wiping the tears from my cheeks, I went to Tristian, whispering nonsense words so he would loosen his grip enough that I could help him. After wrapping his eyes, I grabbed his arm to bring him deeper into the shadow of the tree where the sun's rays couldn't blind us.

"What was that?" he hoarsely asked.

"It was the sun. We've been in the dark so long it will take time for our eyes to adjust to the light."

"Are you sure that they'll adjust?"

"Absolutely. It will just take a bit of time," I confidently told him, even though it was just a guess, one that I hoped was right.

Standing up, he held his hand out to me. "Come on, we need to go and get our packs before something happens to them."

Taking his hand, I allowed him to lead me back to our packs, exactly where we left them. But instead of staying there, he picked them up and took us back to the shady spot by the water that we had just left. "It's better if we stay out of the sun as much as possible for now, until we know the effects that it will have on our bodies," he said, before sitting back down and pulling out breakfast for us.

I couldn't argue with him; he made perfect sense. If the sun did this to our eyes, there was no telling what it would do to our skin. Reaching for the food he set out for me, I slowly ate it as I looked around this place, no less lovely even with my muted vision.

"Do you think its OK if we explore or should we wait until it gets dark?" I asked, wanting to explore, but willing do what he felt best.

"We'll have to be careful, but I think you're right and we should explore. We need to find food and shelter."

Looking around, I was sure there was an abundance of food; we just had to figure out what was good to eat. "We should watch the animals and see what they eat."

"Yeah, that's probably the best plan. If they're eating it, it should be safe for us."

Looking at the water, I said, "Do you think it would be OK if I went into the water?"

"I think so, why?"

Smiling, I picked at my clothing with my fingers. "Because I stink and I want to feel what it's like," I said, looking at it longingly. Water had always been scarce for us, we were allotted a certain amount each day. No one had ever submersed themselves in it in our cavern, but I knew that that's the way we used to bathe.

Laughing, he said, "Yeah, you are ripe!"

Ignoring him, I started to strip, eager to go in. Leaving on my underclothes, I grabbed the bar of soap that my sisters had covetously guarded like it was food. Pushing away the memories of them and the pain it brought, I gathered up my clothes and approached the edge. Setting the clothes down, I timidly set my foot on a rock that was in the water. It was the strangest feeling. It was warm and cold if that makes any sense. Intrigued, I stepped on another rock, then another, until water moved around my legs, all the way up to my knees. Shivering from the chill of the water, but warmed from the sun, I was entranced by the feelings. The water was a clear color I had never seen the likes of, ours had always had a brown tinge to it.

Knowing that if I thought about it too much I'd never do it, I jumped from a rock into the darker, deeper part in front of me. Squeezing my eyes and mouth closed, I sank down, my head going completely under and it was terrifying until my feet touched the ground. Laughing when I broke back to the surface, I gave a little scream when Tristian put his arm around me.

"Are you alright?" he frantically demanded, pulling me toward the rock I had just jumped from.

Giggling, I said, "I'm fine, I just forgot to put my feet down." I stood and the water came to my shoulders. "Isn't it the most amazing thing that you've ever felt?" I babbled. Giddy as I moved through it, I dunked my head back under, trying to touch the bottom with my hand.

Coming back up, spitting out the water that was in my mouth, I guessed I should keep it closed down there. I found Tristian were I left him, but he had smile on his face when he looked at me. Shaking his head, he grabbed my soap off the rock, turning his back.

Not about to let him ruin my fun, I moved my arms, kicking and splashing, trying to teach myself something I once read about—swimming. I was just getting the hang of it when he grabbed my foot, pulling me toward him. Sputtering at his unintentional dunking, I didn't get a chance to say anything. I had just opened my mouth to let him have it when he grabbed my hand and placed the soap in it before turning and going toward the shore. Sticking my tongue out at his retreating back, I hurried and cleaned myself, wanting to get back to my fun. I had never felt freedom before, the joy of no responsibilities, and I wanted to bask in it for as long as I could.

Unfortunately Tristian had other ideas. When I went to put the soap on the rock, I saw him by the edge of the water cleaning his clothes without the soap—he was just wetting them. I guess playtime was over. Climbing out of the water, I gathered my clothes and went over to him. We silently worked together until everything was clean, laying the clothes out in the sun to dry before going back to sit in our shaded haven. After a while, I realized that my skin wasn't cooling down. I thought that it was being in the sun that was making it warm, but as I looked down at it, I realized it was pink and it was starting to hurt. Looking over to Tristian, I saw that he was in the same condition.

"Do you feel OK?" I asked.

"No, my skin hurts and I feel tired," he yawned

"Me too. Do you think that being in the sun did this?" I asked, pointing at the redness.

"It must have, we're going to have to be careful about being in it for any length of time. I think it's also best if we keep our skin covered by our clothing if we have to be in it."

Nodding that I agreed, I let out a yawn and laid down on the cool grass. It felt good against my warm skin. I must have fallen asleep, because when I opened my eyes again, it was just getting darker. My skin still hurt, though not as bad, and so did my head. Tristian was spread out next to me and our clothes were in a pile next to of him, he must have gathered them up before going to sleep. Standing up, I was a little dizzy, but I fought it until my head cleared.

Removing the strips of cloth from my eyes, I looked down at my skin. It was looking much better, though it was still red in some spots like burns. Taking a long drink of water to clear my head, I quietly dressed, wanting to give him as much time to rest as I could.

A sound I thought never to hear again echoed in the distance, causing me to run to Tristian and shake him awake. Terrified, I put my hand over his mouth as it sounded again, causing him to sit up. With wide eyes we looked around, waiting to see the soldiers come for us. Jumping to his feet, Tristian grabbed his clothing, throwing them on as I stuffed everything else back into our bags. A third shot rang out just as I put the last item into the bag; throwing myself to the ground, I waited for our deaths.

"It's too far away," Tristian whispered.

Confused, I asked. "What's too far away?"

"The sound, listen, it's carrying over the land. They're not shooting at us, but something else."

Well, that was great, but then who were they shooting at? "We're not alone up here," I said, as things we had seen since the moment we entered the Cavern of Death began to click in my head. Things like empty abandoned homes. But then I began to think of other things that I had never thought to question before, like our Governors' and speakers' skin color on the day of the lottery, at times darker than ours, but at other times red like mine was now. How many years had they been on the surface, leaving us to the darkness below? How many of us had they kept killing instead of finding a new food source that seemed to grow and walk in abundance upon this land?

As these thoughts rolled through my head, I was no longer scared, I was angry. My anger grew, strengthening my resolve as other thoughts went through me. We were their slaves and masters did not travel without their slaves. Crowley had told me that long ago, he wasn't sure how many hundreds of years ago, one of our jobs used to be traveling to the other caverns to serve as house servants, but the practice was done away with and no one knew why. As of this moment I knew why. It was because they couldn't have us going back and telling our community that the world had healed and we could leave the caverns. Oh, I was sure that they still had servants, so they either kept breeding pairs up here or not everyone really died at the lottery. How many of us were up here and where were they?

Turning to Tristian, I said, "We need to know what that was. Who or what they were shooting at."

Staring off into the distance in the direction that the shot came from, he murmured, "If we go and they capture us, we'll be killed." He left out the "eventually," that hung between us, unsaid.

We had just escaped from that hell, I was a fool for wanting to go anywhere near them. It wasn't just my life I was risking, but Tristian's, too. Still, even knowing this, I blurted out, "They won't be expecting anyone else to be out here. If we're careful, they'll never know that we were there and I think it's best if we know where they are and what they're up to."

"I know what you're thinking, Misty, and the chances that she'll be there are next to none," he guessed, turning his gaze to me. Closing my eyes, I wanted to deny it, but I couldn't. I knew that there was next to no chance that Rose was there, but still, until I saw for myself, it would haunt me. Every time I closed my eyes, she would join the twins, cursing me for leaving them behind, for not saving them.

With a sigh, he said, "We'll cross the water here where it's shallow and make our way toward the higher ground over there. It'll give us a better lay of the land, so we know what we're walking into."

Raising my gaze to his, I whispered, "Thank you," letting out a breath that I hadn't realized I had been holding.

Reaching out, I took his offered hand, allowing him to pull me up. Silently I let him lead me across the water and into the woods. The sun was moving lower in the sky as we made our way. Fading rays from the sun penetrated the woods, giving it a soft glow that was magical. The darker it became, the more alive the woods became, as animals moved around. Their sounds seemed to carry into the night from soft hoots to sinister howls that caused shivers to race down my spine. Moving into a small clearing, Tristian stopped me from moving on by grabbing my arm.

"We'll camp here for the night; it's too dark to safely keep moving on," he said, dropping his pack, "grab some sticks to make a small fire, it seems colder here than by the water."

Gathering the sticks in the clearing, I asked worriedly, "Do you think a fire is a good idea, someone might see it?"

"It'll be fine, I'll keep it small. The shots we heard were miles away, echoing from the distance."

"Are you sure? I'm not cold. I think we would be OK without one."

Throwing the sticks he had gathered down in the middle of the clearing, he used some dried leaves and got the fire going. "It's not the cold that I'm worried about keeping away, but the animals," he said, taking the sticks from my hands before pulling me down next to him.

Taking out the food and water, he split up a small portion between us before putting the pitiful amount left back. We would have to find something soon or we would starve. It would be a true irony if we managed to starve in a place where food literally grew around us after staying alive so long in the cavern.

Breaking the silence, I asked, "You think this is foolish, don't you?"

"For thinking that you might find Rose, yes, for wanting to know where their city is so we can avoid it, no," he quietly answered.

"It's not that I think she's alive, it's having to know that she's dead," I said, trying to find the right words. "Besides, aren't you curious to know if there are others of us among them?"

Seeming to think on my words before he answered, he said, "I don't know if it will be better or worse to know. If they're there we can't help them and I will have to live with that knowledge that we are free while they are slaves. But if they aren't there I know that they suffer below, trapped in darkness while their tormentors walk in paradise." Gazing at his profile, I watched as he searched the fire, as if expecting it to hold the answers to his torment. I thought about what he said and knew that it was true. If I found Rose, I couldn't take her from there and if I didn't find her, I knew that death had claimed her—either way, it would haunt me, the inability to do anything. Whether I was free out here or a slave within the caverns didn't matter. I still didn't have the power to do what mattered. So I suppose the question was, is it better to live in ignorance or wallow in regret?

Unable to stand the dark thoughts that I held no answer to a moment longer, I banished them to the back of my mind. Reaching into my bag, I pulled out the strips of cloths and tied them around my eyes, not wanting to wake in pain again. Stretching out onto the ground facing the fire, I closed my eyes, forcing sleep to take me. At some point in the night, Tristian joined me, laying down behind me and wrapping his arm around me. I woke slightly as he raised my head to pillow it on the crook of his arm before his gentle murmurs lulled me back to sleep.

I don't know how long we slept before a sound woke me. Opening my eyes to pitch darkness, the fire having died long ago, I slowly raised my hand and removed the bindings from my eyes. Something wasn't right. I could feel the tiny hairs on the back of my neck standing up as if someone was watching me. The tightening of Tristin's arm around me would have caused me to jump if I hadn't been holding myself so stiffly. He obviously must have heard the sound and woken also. The flash of the knife in his hand by my head gave me comfort even as I cursed myself for not taking my knife from my bag before I laid down.

A rustling in the thicket started again as if something within was moving toward us. When I felt

Tristian move, so did I. Slowly mirroring his movement, we rose to a crouch on the balls of our feet. Luckily my bag was within my reach, and inching my hand in, I felt the handle of my knife not a moment too soon. A deep growling sound began to echo in the silence before shining eyes gazed out at us in menace. A large chasm surrounded by sharp white teeth moved from the greenery, the figure it was attached to was huge, and massive paws shook the ground as it came into our small clearing. Pawing the ground, it twisted its head as it rose into the air, towering over our small forms before coming back down with a heavy thump and a roar of challenge that was unmistakable.

Tristian's "RUN!" broke through my terror at the sight before us. With a tight grip on my bag, I followed him into the darkened woods, swinging my bag onto my back as we went. The monster pursued us, the sound of heavy braches breaking in its wake. We could hear it closing in; turning and twisting through the woods was no use—it still followed. Terrified, we came to a large tree, and gripping its limbs, we pulled ourselves up. Higher and higher we climbed, but what we hadn't counted on was the fact that the beast would follow. We were halfway up into the tree when it found us, digging its sharp claws into the tree trunk as it pulled itself up. Trapped in the high branches, we watched in horror as it made its way toward us, growling and snapping as it went. We had only one choice: to keep going up. The branches got thinner and weaker the higher we went, cracking under the pressure of our weight at times. We had reached the top with nowhere to go, the monster right under us shaking the tree with each swipe it took at us. My back was to the trunk of the tree with Tristian in front of me, trying to offer what little protection that he could when the rope end coming out of his bag gave me an idea.

Pulling out the rope while trying to hold on to him and the tree so we wouldn't topple to our deaths was what saved us. The tree began to shudder so badly I thought we were going to topple out, causing me to drop part of the rope to get a better grip on Tristian. The rope coil fell into the monster's face, startling it. When it swiped at the rope, the thing lost its balance, putting too much weight on a weak branch, causing it to fall to the ground. The sound of breaking branches on the way down signaled that its fall was slow enough that when it hit the ground it sat there stunned instead of dead for a moment before yelping and running back into the darkness that it had come from. Wide-eyed, we gazed at where the monster retreated, waiting for it to come back. Every sound that I heard caused fear to engulf me until about an hour passed without any sight of it.

"I think it's alright to get down, I don't think it's coming back," Tristian whispered to me.

Furiously shaking my head, I said, "I'm not going back down there until the sun comes up."

"Alright, let's move down to the larger branches that we can sit on, we'll sleep up here for the rest of the night," he said, while prying the rope from my hand so he could roll it back up.

Taking slow breaths, I calmed myself enough to take the rope from him and put it back in his bag. Telling me to stay, he began to descend first before motioning me to join him. We went about halfway down before he was satisfied with a branch. Taking his pack off, he took out the rope and looped it around the tree before telling me to take my bag off and pulling me into his lap. Cradling me to his chest, he tied the rope around us and the bags before taking the forgotten cloth from around my neck and recovering my eyes. Wrapping my arms around him, I listened to the beat of his heart until the sun started to rise and exhausted sleep finally claimed me.

Chapter 10

It's been five sun risings since the monster attacked us from the darkness. The first day after the attack, every sound in the woods had me gripping my knife. We had climbed carefully from our tree and backtracked to our original camp, the damage from the night before making it easy to find. The few items that we had left behind after our mad dash, we gathered. After carefully studying the paw prints left behind so we knew to avoid an area if we saw them again, we set out quickly moving through the area, not wanting to meet up with the animal again. Since that night, we had made sure to either find high ground or a tree to sleep in, not wanting to be caught at even level like that again.

About two days into our trek, we ran out of food. Worried, we slowed down to search the area for animal trails. We were lucky we only had to go a day before we stumbled onto deer eating a black type of berry. Greedily, we stuffed our mouths before we stuffed our bags full and moved on. We had managed to stumble onto other types of fruit and nuts I recognized from pictures at school, collecting them as we went, but I was leery of the berries, preferring to avoid them if I didn't see an animal eating them first.

Our eyes seemed to be adjusting to the sun a little at a time. This morning before we left, I was able to remove one on the pieces of cloths and still see without pain. If we're lucky, within a month we won't need them at all. Looking ahead, I couldn't help but smile in relief as the place where Tristian had been leading us was finally coming into view. I couldn't help but be a little worried as we approached, since after the night of the attack he had been more serious than I have ever seen him. Specifically, he was worried about me. He wouldn't let me go first, but pushed me behind him, taking the lead. I knew he wasn't getting enough rest, but when I offered to stay up while he slept, he ignored me. We were going to have to find somewhere safe to hole up for a few days before he drops from exhaustion.

Wanting to distract him, I smiled when heard a stream off to the side. Running forward, I grabbed his hand pulling him to a stop. "Do you hear that?"

Running a weary hand across his face, he said, "Do I hear what, the water?"

Nodding my head, I tugged on his arm. "Come on, we need to fill our bottles and I want to try swimming again."

Moving in front of me, he kept hold of my hand, but changed direction to the sound of the water. When we reached its banks, I stood frozen, caught by the beauty. It was different from the other one. This one has a ledge that water was falling off from above that almost made it look like a moving blanket. Thick groups of brightly colored flowers coated both sides of it, giving it a magically quality. Entranced, I began pulling my clothes off, dropping them as I walked, wanting to be part of the beauty. Between the shade of the trees and the lowness of the sun in the sky, I carefully took off my eye wraps. When I get only a slight sting, I discarding them completely, dropping them with my clothes before stepping in.

The water was colder here than in the other stream, but I ignored it as I walked toward the cascading water from above. Tentatively reaching out, I was fascinated as it slid over my skin. Closing my eyes, I stepped forward and let it cover me, amazed that it was not as cold as the water below. Wherever it was coming from must have been heated by the sun. Running my hands over my face, I lifted my chin up, pushing my hair back. For long minutes I stood there before arms encircled me from behind, startling me into turning. Placing my hands onto the bare, water-covered chest to hold my balance, a shiver passed through me as I collected my courage. Forcing my gaze up, I was caught in the same trance that this place had put over me. With shallow breaths, I stayed locked in his arms as he bent and captured my lips. Like before, I was shocked for a moment, but unlike before I couldn't pull away, caught in his arms I felt the warmth of what he was doing to my lips spread through me. Pressing into his body instead of away, I curled my fingers into his chest, wanting him closer but instead it pushed him away. Breaking our kiss, he turned me in his arms, keeping my back pressed tightly to his chest. Wanting more, I tried to turn back, but he held me still, not allowing it. If it wasn't for his unsteady breaths, I would have thought that he was unaffected.

His chin, which had been resting on my head, slid down the side of my face until his lips came to on my neck. With a barely-there touch, he pressed them to me, whispering, "Close your eyes and don't move," before removing them and dropping his arms. Tight with nerves, I jumped a little when his hand glided up my neck, tilting my head back. The smell of soap touched my nose as his hands

140

moved through my hair, washing it. I don't ever remember anyone ever washing my hair before, but even if they had I don't think it felt like this. I was shaking with emotions that I couldn't identify by the time he finished. He told me to turn and I slowly did as he asked. Dumbly, I stared at my hand that he placed the soap in as I watched him kneel down in front of me, pressing his face into my stomach. Raising my shaking hands, I slowly soaped them up before setting the soap on a shelf of rocks next to me. With study movements, I worked my fingers through his hair as his hot short gasps against my stomach caused it to quiver. Placing a hand on each side of his head I gently tilted it back until hot eyes gazed at me before closing as the falling water and my fingers softly rinsed out the soap.

When the last of the soap left him I allowed my fingers to glide down to his shoulders. In silence, he opened his eyes, holding my gaze with his as he rose and stepped back, diving into the cool water and making his way back to shore. Not looking back, he walked onto the bank, collecting his bag and moved into the woods. With shaking hands, I took the soap and finished my bath, waiting as long as I dared before going to the shore. Drying off the best that I could, I pulled my clothes over my damp skin.

Filling my water bottles, I froze when Tristian kneeled down beside me to fill his.

"If we're going to make the high ground before the sun completely sets, we have to get going now," he said, as if nothing had happened, "and don't worry about your eye covers—the sun is down enough that it won't be an issue." He threw this in as an afterthought before turning and walking away.

Shock held me still before anger took over. Fine, if that is what he wanted then we'll just pretend that it never happened. Stuffing my bottle and clothes into my bag, I stood up and followed him, not saying a word at the grueling pace that he set for us to make up for the side trip to the water. It was well dark by the time we reached the spot that he had chosen. Without a word, I dropped my bag to the ground, too tired to be mad, just trying to catch my breath. Once I felt that I wouldn't keel over, I searched the grounds and gathered sticks. The spot we were on was pretty bare, so I had to walk about twenty minutes back the way we came to find what we needed. When I got back with a sack full of sticks it was to find a furious Tristian. "Where have been?" he yelled, knocking the bag from my hands before grabbing my arms to hold me in place.

Confused, I said, "I went to get fuel for the fire."

Too angry to speak at my words, he dragged me toward a group of large boulders that was hiding our fire from view. Pushing me forward, he turned on his heels and walked away. Completely irritated by his high-handed attitude, I turned right on my heels to follow him.

Grabbing his arm to stop him, I said, "What's your problem?!"

Instead of pulling his arm from me, he moved forward, crowding my space. "Go back to the fire," he pushed out between clenched teeth, before pulling his arm from my grip, intending to walk away.

Who the hell did he think I was? A child to be spoken to that way?

"From the way you're behaving wandering off without telling me, that's exactly what I think you're acting like," he growled, forcing me to realize that I had said that out loud. Taking a deep breath, I gave him a withering look before turning on my heels and going back to the fire. Obviously not liking being ignored, he stomped behind, towering over me as I sat down and stared into the fire. "Don't walk away from me when I'm speaking to you."

Ignoring him, I kept looking into the fire until he knelt down and gripped my face, forcing me to look at him. Keeping my eyes adverted to over his shoulder, I shed my face of expression and said in a monotone, "I'm just doing what you told me, sitting by the fire like a good girl."

This seemed to drive him over the edge. Pushing me down, he loomed over me, pinning me to the ground. Not wanting to give him the satisfaction, I sat perfectly still as he waited tensely for me to struggle. After a moment, when he realized that I wasn't moving, he gently gripped my face, getting the reaction his anger couldn't—my eyes on his. "I didn't know where you were. I didn't know if you were hurt or if someone or something had taken you." Removing his grip from my face, he gently ran his fingers over my pulse as he continued in the same low voice. "The only thing that I knew is that when I called out you didn't answer or come." Leaning down until his lips touched my ear, he held his weight on his arm, not touching me. "Now do you understand why I was upset with you?"

"Yes," I said breathlessly, unable to hide the reaction to his nearness. Satisfied with my answer, he nimbly jumped up and walked away, leaving me on the ground to fight back my body's traitorous reaction. Staring up at the sky, I tried to figure out how we had gotten to this point. I shook my head as the sky didn't give me the answer as to why I was suddenly attracted to my best friend. I rolled to my side, gazing at the fire, no longer hungry. I closed my eyes and fell into a light sleep. Turning in my sleep, I snuggled deeper into the warmth, wiggling and moving trying to get comfortable until hard hands forced me still. Whimpering, I raised my arms, wiping my bleary eyes before blinking them into focus. Tristian's face was level with mine. Softened by sleep, it looked like the boy I had always known. Careful not to wake him, I scooted out of his arms, going over to restart the fire. Not wanting to go back to sleep until I knew that it would stay lit, I walked around the boulders to stretch my legs.

At first when I looked into the distance I thought that the sun was rising. My sleepy mind was not making sense of what I was seeing. As I kept looking I realized what I was seeing were lights in the distance covering a huge expanse of area. The more I focused, the more I thought I saw outlines of buildings, but with the distance it could have just been shadows playing tricks on my mind. Sitting down, I stared. So that was the city. Looking around the surrounding areas, I saw no other lights like that, so it must be the only one. The distance from us was great, it could take us weeks, months to reach it, depending on the terrain we encountered. Now that we knew where it was, wouldn't it just be smarter to head in another direction and move away from it?

What would we really find there that would make a difference to us? Did deep down I think that we could help those people? There were two of us and what were there, hundreds of thousands, millions of them waiting for their chance to kill us for daring to escape the caverns? Standing up I made my way back to Tristian, sitting down next to him, glad that he was finally sleeping. Our earlier fight must have worn him out. Carefully reaching my hand out, I lightly touched his cheek. My thoughts were going to our future. The weather up here in the world above was different than the cavern and always changing. We had no clue when it would change or how. We should be worrying about a permanent shelter to retreat to and stocking supplies before even thinking of making our journey to the Loyalist city. Deciding to talk with him in the morning about this, I turned and added more wood to the fire. Once I was sure that it would go for a while, I laid back down next to Tristian. For a moment I was afraid that I had awakened him, when his arm snaked out and pulled me into his embrace, but when he didn't move after that and his even breathing was the only thing that I heard, I closed my eyes and joined him.

Opening my eyes, I blinked at my fuzzy vision until I realized that the cloths were over them. Tristian must have put them on was the only thing my sleepy mind could surmise as I thought of the night before. Stretching slowly, I looked around for him and when I couldn't see him I rose. Moving around the boulders, I saw him sitting in the same spot I was last night, gazing out at the city that was barely visible in the distance. Without a word, I sat down next to him resting my head on his shoulder, smiling when he put his arm around me. Sitting there, my thoughts of last night came to me again.

Breaking the silence, I said, "I was thinking that I was wrong. Maybe we shouldn't go to the city." When he remained quiet, I said, "I was thinking that for now we should be working on finding a shelter somewhere and collecting food. We don't know the weather patterns of this place. Eventually we need to journey to the city, but until we have a home base, I don't know if it's a good idea.

"Are you sure?" he asked, those three little words telling me he would risk death to the elements if it would make me happy.

Nodding my head against his shoulder, I asked, "Which way do you think we should go?"

Looking around, he gave a humorous laugh. "That way toward the mountains. We'll probably do best in a cave since we don't have any tools."

Unfortunately, he was right. Until we could make or find tools, we were pretty limited in our forms of shelter. As much as I hated the thought of living in a cave even for a short time, it was probably our best bet at survival. "OK, a cave it is," I said, trying to put enthusiasm in my voice. From his dry chuckle I knew that he wasn't buying it.

Looking at where he pointed, I was a little worried because it was definitely far from the city, but closer than I liked it to be. "Are you sure we shouldn't look around before settling on the first mountain we see?"

"You never took me as the type of girl who would want a bigger mountain."

"Smart ass."

"Well, if we're going to get there, we'd better get moving," he announced, no more trilled with the idea than I was.

Ugh. Getting up, I grabbed my stuff, hoping that we weren't making a mistake, and followed him. Smiling to myself, I realized all the time we were children he followed me, trying to keep me out of trouble and now here I was following him with no hopes of keeping either of us out of trouble.

The closer we moved toward the mountain, the farther away it seemed. Every night we fell to the ground exhausted, we weren't even lighting fires any longer. A few days back, we had been blocked by a large ravine, water raging loudly deep within it. We spent hours moving along it, trying to find a narrow part to cross with our ropes, and instead we found a beautiful stone bridge to carry us across. In the middle of the mass of wilderness stood signs of human life and though Tristian hadn't said anything, I knew that it worried him as much as it had me. We had assumed that the Loyalists stayed within the city, but this bridge proved that someone came out this far. Far enough that they built a bridge large and strong enough to carry vehicles across with ease. The only comfort that I had was that the bridge appeared old and I didn't see any recent tracks, though it was defiantly maintained and in good repair.

Strange things had been happening ever since we had crossed the bridge. I suppose "happening" isn't the right word, it's more like a strange feeling had descended over us. A feeling of being watched and judged. The closer we came to the mountain, the more it seemed to creep over me. At night when we slept, I could almost swear that I heard whispered conversations around us. During the day, the woods seemed almost eerily silent, as if they were waiting for something. We had been walking most of the day when we came across a small stream and decided to take a rest.

Tired, I dropped my bag and took off my shoes before wading my way into the stream and sitting on a boulder. Even with how tired I was, my gaze kept searching the woods as I absently touched the knife at my side, something that I had carried on me without fail since we were attacked that night. A small movement to my side caught my eye and turning to it, I was frozen in shock. A little face peeked out at me from behind a tree, smiling and giving me a wave of her fingers when she saw that she had my attention. Tearing my gaze from her, I slowly stood up, my gaze searching the shore as I backed up to get to Tristian.

My foot had just touched the shore when I felt his hand wrap around my wrist. Turning my gaze to him I found myself staring at his back. I tried to take a step to the side, but he tightened his grip, silently telling me to stay behind him. Rising to my toes I saw what held him so still. About twenty men and women stood in front of us with more coming out of the woods behind them. A woman separated herself from the group and stepped forward, holding her hands out in a peaceful gesture. Looking to the others with her, I saw that they were armed, but made no move to reach for their weapons as they gazed at us.

The woman stopped walking when she was halfway between her people and us. "We mean you no harm, please put away your knife before someone gets hurt."

Since my knife wasn't out that meant Tristian's was. Ignoring the tightening of his grip I kept my body close to his, but moved it around so that I was next to him instead of behind him. Reaching out slowly, I covered the hand holding the knife, gently pressing it down. If these people wanted us dead, they would have done it by now and there was no way to escape them. We were surrounded. But instead of saying that, I whispered, "They have children with them," hoping he would understand what I meant.

After a moment's hesitation, he sheathed his knife. "Who are you?" he asked the woman as she lowered her hands.

"My name is Mayla and we live in the village ahead." Seeing the fear that flashed through our eyes, she shook her head vigorously and hurried to explain. "We are not from the City to the West, we will not harm you"

Finding my voice, I said, "I don't understand. If you did not come from the city, then where did you come from?"

Instead of answering me, she said, "You are welcome to come with us to our village. You were headed that way anyway," she smiled, pointing toward our original destination. "We have been watching you to make sure that you had not come from the city. We know now that you are not Hunters, but Prey, and are welcome to come."

What the hell did she mean "Prey"? Opening my mouth to ask her, I was cut off when she started walking to the water, giving us a wide berth as the people behind her followed and crossed the water, joining the child I had seen on the other side. Keeping them in our sight, we watched them until they disappeared into the woods.

"What is going on?" I asked in confusion, not expecting an answer.

"I don't know, but gather your things, we're leaving," Tristian said. Moving around, I put my shoes back on and picked up my bag, surprised when Tristian stopped me from crossing the water. "What do you think you're doing?" he demanded. "I said that we were leaving."

Wait, what? "I thought you meant that we were going to their village."

"Are you crazy, we have no idea who those people are or what they want and you just think where going to walk into there?" he said, looking at me as if I had finally cracked.

Rolling my eyes, I said, "Tristian, listen to me, those people, whoever they are, have information that we need." Seeing that he wasn't impressed with my words, I tried a different tack. "They could have killed us at any time, so they obviously don't mean to hurt us or force us to go with them." When I saw the grudging admittance of that flash in his eyes, I pushed forward. "We have no idea how to survive on the surface and obviously they do. Even if we don't stay with them, they'll have tools that we will need to survive." When I saw him close his eyes and heard his long, drawn-out sigh, I knew that I had him. Hiding my smile, knowing that he wouldn't appreciate it, I kept my eyes cast down as he pulled me across the water.

Chapter 11

We saw no one for two hours, though we felt their eyes on us watching. Our first look at their world was breathtaking. There was a very large valley at the base of the mountain filled with buildings of all shapes and sizes. But it was what you saw when you looked at the mountain itself that was astounding. Huge figures and designs were carved right into the mountain surrounding a large entrance that people moved through, going and coming from the town below. Vehicles like I had never seen before moved on roadways heading in and out of the valley from all directions. As we moved closer, the sound of children's laughter echoed from a large spot that they played at where there were all sort of strange things that they climbed and swung on.

"It looks just like the movies that she used to show us," I whispered, thinking of the treat that the teacher would give us if we behaved. An old movie that had been passed through her family. This is the world we were meant to live in.

Squeezing my hand, Tristian pulled me nearer to him as we saw the child and the woman from the water. Smiling to us, they waited patiently for us to join them.

Once we almost reached them, the child broke away, coming to me and grabbing my free hand. "Come on," she said, smiling and pulling me forward.

"I'm sorry, Helen has been impatient for your arrival, wishing to show you off to her friends." The pretty dark-haired woman said, smiling down at the child. "But she understands that it must wait for a bit until after you are settled and we answer each other's questions. Don't you?"

Turning big eyes up, she said, "Yes, Mama, I understand."

Turning her gaze back to us, Mayla said, "Please follow me, we will get you settled before we eat."

Letting go of the little girl's hand, who immediately grabbed a surprised Tristian's, I moved up to walk next to Mayla. "I'm sorry we have been rude, it's just that we never expected to find people like you. My name is Misty and that is Tristian."

Smiling at me, she said, "We know. The others having been following you for days."

"Why were they following us?" I asked, ignoring the creepy "We know."

Frowning, she answered, "To make sure that you were not Hunters."

OK, now here is something that I definitely wanted to understand. "What are Hunters?"

Changing her frown to one of confusion, she asked, "Are you not Prey?"

"Mayla, I have no idea what you are talking about."

Stopping, she turned and looked at me. "If you are not Hunters or Prey, then where did you come from?"

Seeing that she was truly baffled by us, I said, "We escaped from the caverns," watching her reaction.

"I don't understand, what caverns?"

She really had no idea about the caverns or she didn't realize what I meant. Glancing at Tristian, I got his slight nod. Talking slowly, I tried to explain it in a way for her to understand. "The caverns that the survivors went to after the government destroyed the surface of this planet during the last great revolution. Where we are forced to live to this day as slaves for them."

I watched as what I said sank in. "But that's impossible," she whispered in denial, "all know that only those that live within the city besides us survived the great destruction." Strengthening her voice, she said, "Yes, you are mistaken, you must be Prey from the city and are just confused," turning and walking ahead.

Catching up with her, I grabbed her arm to stop her. "Mayla, have you ever heard of the caverns before? Have the Prey every spoken of it?"

"Most of the Prey we save do not survive long, they are too injured or weak. The few that have survived have never mentioned the caverns before. I know of them because of our history discs, these lessons are taught to our children at school," she said, smiling sadly at me.

Seeing that this was upsetting her, I said, "I don't want to hold you up. Let's go get settled, then we'll speak."

I could see she was still troubled by my words, but she nodded her head and led the way to a large building. I was glad when she opened the door for us to enter, but the stares that we were getting weren't helping my nerves. Taking us to an elevator, we entered and rode several floors up into the building. Stopping at the eighth floor, we got off and followed her through a long corridor lined with doors until we reached one at the end. Opening it, she led us into a large home.

Smiling, though not as brightly as before, she said, "This is where you will stay for now. Please use anything you wish, everything has been placed here for your use." Moving to the table in the center of the room, she said, "If you place a drop of this solution in each eye, it will clear them so that the sun will no longer bother you." Opening her mouth as if to say something, she stopped, taking a deep breath before continuing. "I hope it is alright to dine here with you for today. Some of our people wish to speak with you and I thought that you would be more comfortable here"—waiting for our nods, she continued—"we will eat in three hours. I will see you then. Come, Helen," she said, before hurrying out of the room and leaving us alone.

Walking around, it was like nothing I had ever seen before—bright colors and different textures were everywhere. Moving into the room off to the side, I saw that it was a bedroom. A large bed stood in the center of the room, looking soft like a cloud. Moving around, I found a closet full of clothing and a large bathroom. This place could have fit my old home inside it three times over. Feeling uncomfortable, I went back to the main room.

"What do you think, Tristian?"

Looking as uncomfortable as I felt, he said, "About what, this place or Mayla?" Sitting down on the couch, he asked, "I don't know, why they would take us in like this?"

"I know, I guess the only thing we can do is wait until dinner to find out what they want in return for this," I said, looking around at the beautiful room then down at myself. "I think we should go and get cleaned up for dinner. They left clothing in the closets for our use." Walking over to the room I just left, I quietly closed the door and began to prepare for the trial ahead.

Putting it off for as long as I dared, I exited the bedroom feeling more self-conscious than I had ever been in my life. A dress had been laid out on the bed when I came out of the bathroom. I had never worn one before, but I guess that this was what you wore to dinner here. It was a deep green that matched my eyes and it fell to my feet. The material felt as soft as the petals of a flower and moved around me as I walked. I put on the matching shoes with little jewels gracing my feet and left my hair down, not knowing what else to do with it.

Quietly opening my door, I found Tristian where I left him, sitting on the couch with his back to me, except he was bathed and in fresh clothing. Walking out, the smell of food caught my attention as a girl stepped forward. "May I get you a drink, Miss?" she asked.

"Um, no thank you, I'm fine" I said, before turning back to Tristian. He was no longer sitting but standing looking at me as if he had never seen me before. Caught in his gaze I don't know how long, we would have stood like that forever if a knock at the door hadn't broken our concentration. The girl who offered me a drink walked by and opened the door, letting in the small group of people waiting on the other side. Before I had a chance to get uncomfortable with their obvious appraisal of me, I felt Tristian move to my side. I smiled at Mayla, the only face in the group we recognized, and she moved forward to stand at my other side.

"Tristian, Misty, please allow me to make introductions." Motioning to a tall, dark-haired man in a uniform, she said, "This is Johnathon, our head of security. The man to his right is Marcus, our local Council

Representative." Turning me a little from the short, portly man, she continued, "The lady right there is Evelyn, Marcus's wife, and last but not least this is Peter, a good friend of mine and our head historian," she finished, indicating the older tall man pushing up his glasses.

Murmuring our hellos, we followed Mayla's lead when she motioned us all to the table. Everyone remained quiet as the two girls moved around the table serving us. The food they put in front of us were things I had never seen before, delicious smells rose from each as they uncovered them. Smiling, the two girls stepped forward, whispering in my ear as they placed a little of each thing on my plate, letting me know what it was. When they were finished, they went back a few feet and just stood there waiting for us to eat. Confused, it took me a moment to realize that they weren't going to join us. Unable to back to hold back my anger, I said, "I didn't realize that you kept slaves."

Four shocked expressions turned to look at me. "These girls aren't slaves, they work here. We don't keep slaves," Mayla said, the first to find her voice.

"Then why aren't they joining us?" I demanded, not believing a word coming out of her mouth.

"Because they work here," she said, puzzled at the anger she could see of my face.

"Are they allowed to leave when they wish and stop working here at any time?" I asked, still suspicious.

Before Mayla could answer me, one of the girls stepped forward, smiling, "This is a job for us, we're paid weekly for it and are able to quit at any time and go find work elsewhere. We're not forced to be here," she said, as the other girl nodded, looking confused.

Letting out a breath, I could feel my cheeks turning pink, but I kept Mayla's gaze, "I'm sorry if I insulted you, but I had to be sure that you weren't the same. I'll die before I live like that again," I venomously told her, wanting there to be no misunderstanding.

"We had heard from Prey that escaped the city's Hunters that they were kept as servants, but they never reacted as you have," the thin man named Peter said, speaking at me as if I was slow. "So we are sorry that no one informed you that the indentured servitude system is not in use here," he explained, smiling at me as if I was a child.

"I don't believe I said 'indentured servitude,' but 'slaves,' and as I told Mayla, we do not come from the city. We have never seen the city. We did not know of its existence until recently," I told him coldly, annoyed at his superior attitude.

Making a scoffing sound it his throat, he said, "If you didn't come from the city, then where did you come from, under a rock?"

Placing a hand on my shoulder, Tristian stopped the blistering retort that I was going to deliver. Looking over to him, I saw the hardened look he speared Paul with before speaking. "As a matter of fact, we did crawl out from under a rock." Seeing the disbelieving look, he continued. "Or to be more precise, we crawled through them. Since the day the government let loose the cleansing upon this land, our people have been kept deep within caverns below the surface as slaves. Generation upon generation have been born, worked, and died in those caverns. Slaves to a system that caters to the Loyalists and their needs." Holding up his hand, stopping Peter's interruption, he said, "Each year we have a lottery as a form of population control. All those but a select few Contributors in their twenty-first year are put to death. We recently learned that it was a lie, along with many other things. Until the day we crawled from a hole and saw the sky, we believed that the world above was still uninhabitable. We took a chance and barely managed to escape the cavern, losing her two sister in the process."

"You're survivors of the Cavern of Death," the man named Johnathon said in disbelief. "It's real."

With wide eyes, I turned and looked at him—he knew. "How do you know about the Cavern of Death?" I whispered, unsure if I wanted the answer, but needed to know.

"Some Prey spoke of it when we first found them in their delirium, but once they were healed they never mentioned it again. We always thought it was just delusions and dismissed it," he said, staring at Tristian and I with a strange look. "But it's true?"

"Yes, we come from the caverns below, but they aren't all called the Cavern of Death. The Cavern of Death is where you go during your twenty-first year—" stopping, I looked to Tristian, wondering how much to tell him. After a hard look at the man, he turned and gave me a small nod. "We always believed that the Cavern of Death is where you went to die, but recently we learned that there is much more to it than that," I said, then stopped, looking at the rapt expressions that surrounded us, and took a deep breath. "We were always told that there was a minimum amount of room, so as our punishment for the uprising, we were forced to death at our twenty-first year. The truth we learned was that there are hundreds of caves below, most filled with hundreds of thousands of our people. Early after we were forced below, the animals died from a disease and could not be regrown, which left the Loyalists with a limited food source." Closing my eyes, I allowed a shudder to pass through me before opening them and staring right into Johnathon's. "So they found a new protein source. It was decided that resources were wasted upon us and that we grew useless as we aged. A young workforce to see to their needs was more preferable. After the animals' death, the Cavern of Death was started and so was a new meat source," I finished, watching as he realized the truth behind my words. Disbelief followed by disgust then horror crossed his face as he gazed into my eyes.

"You're lying, the caverns were emptied hundreds of years ago when the city dwellers came to the surface and built their homes there," Peter said, gazing at me in disgust. "Do you think making up stories about where you came from will make thing easier for you? We told you that we don't believe in indentured servitude."

"Yes, the caverns were emptied of our government and its Loyalists hundreds of years ago," I yelled, slamming my hand on the table, "but not the Contributors––we are kept below as slaves and food."

Shocked silence filled the room at my declaration. Whatever Peter the historian was about to say was silenced with a slashing gesture from Johnathon. Rising from the table, I left my uneaten food and went to the bedroom, slamming the door behind me, trying to regain control of my emotions. That bastard's total dismissal of my words brought images of vacant stares, bodies hanging by hooks. Shuddering at the images, I dropped to my knees as the images became my cousins, their accusing stares. I don't know how long I sat there lost in the horrors of my mind before I felt Tristian's arms around me picking me up and carrying me to the bed. Not letting go, he laid beside me, pulling me tighter as unshed tears burned behind the lids of my eyes.

The room was bathed in total darkness when I finally fought free of the past. "I'm sorry," I whispered, my voice as hoarse as if I had been screaming aloud instead of just in my head.

Squeezing me tightly, he tucked me more firmly under his chin. "Why, it took everything in me not to beat that superior little shit into the ground."

Smiling at the image before the realization of what I had done hit me, I said, "I made this harder for us. They won't accept us after what I did."

"If they won't accept us for you telling the truth, then we don't need to be here." Pulling away to look into my eyes, he said, "It's a large world out there and this is only a small piece of it. We can go anywhere and make a new home." He smiled as he pulled me back into his body.

"Do you think the reason that the others that escaped didn't tell them about us was because they were afraid of their reaction?"

"No, I think they didn't tell them about us because they were cowards," he growled, anger tightening his body.

Rubbing my hand in little circles on his chest, I said, "You see how they reacted, how they looked at us. If it was you and you escaped the city wouldn't you have said nothing, not wanting to jeopardize a future among people who didn't hurt you? Who accepted you and helped you? Wouldn't you want to start a new life where no one knew the horrors of what you had done?"

Releasing me, he rolled to his back, placing his hand over mine, then stopping its movement he stared at the ceiling for long moments before he spoke. "I would have screamed to the heavens the truth of what I knew. I would have told in the hopes that a way could be found to help those still below"—he squeezed my hand to keep me silent—"I found out some things before they left. Johnathon came to me and said that they trade with the city."

Letting his words sink in, a horrible thought came to me. "Do you think that they lied and they really know what goes on within the city?"

"I don't think that the people at the table lied," he slowly said, letting me know that he wasn't sure if someone within this place didn't know or at least suspect the truth.

It they knew the truth, they would want us silenced immediately. If they suspected the truth, they would want the same thing "Is it safe for us to stay here or should we try and leave now?"

Sighing, he said, "For now we stay, at least until we know what's going on in this place. Tomorrow we'll start looking for the truth." Leaning over, he turned off the light next to the bed. "Go to sleep, we're safe enough for tonight."

Closing my eyes, I forced my body to relax into his, even as my mind wouldn't, rushing through the day's events. I was usually so cautious with what I said and did. Now in one moment of abandonment I had thrown my years of caution to the wind and spoken out of turn. The freedom of our time above ground took away my natural caution—I just hoped that I would live to regret my mistake.

Chapter 12

Breakfast was waiting for us on the table when we got up. Fresh fruits and breads with things to spread upon them. The drinks were just as strange. Keely, one of the servers from the night before, was there and explained what everything was. The thing she called coffee was bitter and I would have avoided it if she didn't fix it as she did, adding creams and sugars. It tasted pretty good after she was done. After a few moments, I finally got her to sit with us, and she laughed at my amazement as she explained all the different foods and juices.

I could tell the moment that she got comfortable with us. She started casting us little looks and a blush ran down her cheeks. Taking mercy on her, I said, "You can ask us anything you want."

Blushing even harder, she said, "I'm sorry, I didn't mean to be so obvious."

Smiling, I patted her hand. "It's alright, you can ask us anything you'd like. You've been very kind to us," I said, trying to look nonthreatening.

"It's just that I heard what you said last night. We were told not to talk about it, but I figured since you were the ones that originally said it that it would be OK," Keely stuttered, looking down, unable to hold my eye.

I took a quick look at Tristian before turning back to her. So they were told to keep what we said quiet. "It's perfectly OK to talk to us about it, they just meant not to talk to anyone else," I lied, wanting to find out what she knew.

Seeming relieved at my words, she asked, "I was wondering if what you said was true, are there people really imprisoned below the City to the West?"

"Yes, there are. They're trapped there with no one to help them." I saw in her eyes what she really wanted to ask me. "What I said was true. Everything that I said was true. What I said about the Cavern of Death is true."

With wide eyes she looked at me, I could see a struggle in them before a decision shown in them. "We trade with them, the people from the city."

"How long have you traded with them?"

Glancing around like she expected someone to jump out and stop her, she said, "They came out of the caverns about seven hundred years ago. We stayed away from them because they weren't friendly to us. They built their city then, about two hundred years ago, and we began to trade with them. Little things at first—grains and fruit, until it has become what it is today. A very large commerce between our cities," she whispered.

Her warning was clear. The people profiting from the trades were not going to take kindly to the revelations that our truths could reveal. The sound of the door opening caused us all to jump. Moving away from the table, Keely busied her with her trays while Tristian and I looked down to our plates.

"I'm glad to see you're up," Johnathon said, walking in wearing his uniform. Looking over to Keely, he said, "I'd like to speak with you two privately." Ducking her head, she murmured an excuse and practically ran out the door. Nodding my hello, I quietly sat as Tristian asked him to join us. Glancing at him through my lashes, I wondered if he heard anything. Was he here to see what we knew? Staring at us, he said, "I'd like to speak to you about last night."

"What about last night?" Tristian asked, dropping all pretense.

Nodding his head, he said, "Good, it's better if we don't pretend. I believe what you said last night is true and that's the problem." Holding up his hand, he continued. "Our current government is very much intertwined with the city's. It has, how shall we say, greatly expanded their personal wealth." Watching our faces, he continued. "It's exactly what you are thinking."

"So what do you want us to do, leave?" I asked, already making a list of what to take in my head.

Shaking his head, he said, "Unfortunately, I don't think that's an option at the moment. Marcus who was at dinner last night is deeply intertwined financially with the city and will be reporting what you said. If you tried to leave now, you would be hunted and disposed of."

Closing my eyes in defeat, I knew I had done this. If anything happened to Tristian it would be my fault. "Why are you telling us this? Wouldn't it just be easier for you to kill us if we didn't know it was coming?"

Leaning forward, he said, "Because I have no intention of killing you. In fact I spent all of last night trying to figure out how to keep the two of you alive."

Opening my eyes, I looked at him and saw he truly believed what he was saying, but why? Beating me to the question, Tristian warily asked, "Why would you risk your life for ours, if we're not your people?"

"I would risk my life for yours because you and Misty are more my people than the government I serve," he said, seeing our disbelieving looks. "While I am not a historian, I do know our history and the thing I have noticed the most is that it tends to repeat itself. I'm not alone in being unhappy with the current government and its ties to the City to the West. While it's been many generations since we were forced into the darkness of the caves, our Elders make sure that each generation remembers who put us down there and why it was done. They make sure that we remember that the old government would have rather seen us dead than free. When the representatives from the City to the West come here, they bring their servants and the Elders are quick to remind us that that could easily be us." Taking a drink from the glass in front of him, he rubbed its side, staring in at the contents before continuing. "In the last hundred years, our government has begun to slowly instituting laws that take the people's power away and restrict what is taught within the schools. It's my fear that if something is not done soon it will be as it was before the cleansing. I believe that the City to the West currently controls our officials through their greed and is just waiting for the right moment to strike and seize full control. Their spies are everywhere."

Taking a deep breath, I looked to Tristian—this I could understand. I could understand his willingness to help and trust complete strangers if it meant that his people would be free. Reaching out, I clasped Tristian's hand before turning back to Johnathon. "What do you want us to do?"

The relief in his eyes was easy to see. "Pack your things, we're going to leave here and move you to a safer place. They could make you disappear from here and no one will know, but where I'm taking you, if they tried to harm you there would be rioting in the streets. Your best chance at survival is to make friends fast."

Great, the one thing I'm not good at. Getting up from the table, I hurried into the other room, grabbing our bags and an extra one that I stuffed full of clothing. It's probably best if we blend in. It should make it harder for them to find us. Coming out of the bedroom, I met them by the door. Taking his bag, we waited as Johnathon checked the hall before motioning for us to come out. Moving away down the hall, we just made it inside the stairwell when soldiers began exiting the elevator. Quickly we raced down the stairs and out the back exit to Johnathon's waiting vehicle. Climbing in the back, we hunched down so we wouldn't be seen.

It took several hours to reach our destination. I don't know if that is because it was that far away or because of all the twists and turns we seemed to take. By the time the vehicle stopped, I was stiff from not moving. Getting out, Johnathon came and opened the back door, motioning for us to join him. When we stepped from the vehicle I was surprised to see where we were, not hidden away in some far-off home but in a large village.

Seeing the look on my face, Johnathon smiled at me. "Not what you expected?" Dumbly, I shook my head. "Come on, there are some people I'd like you to meet."

Grabbing my hand, Tristian kept me slightly behind him as he sharply watched our surroundings. Stepping through the doorway of a large building, I blinked to adjust to the dim light. Discreetly placing my hand on the knife that I had hidden at my side, I stepped closer into Tristian's side as the people in the room turned to stare at us.

"Johnathon, what are you doing here?" said a rusty voice to our right that belonged to the oldest man I had ever seen. His body was slightly bent, his beard and hair completely white.

"It's nice to see you, too, Victor," Johnathon smirked, going over to shake his hand.

Completely ignoring the outstretched hand, the old man pulled himself up using a piece of wood as a crutch and hobbled over to me. "Who are you?" he grouched, pulling a smile to my lips. Reaching out my hand, I brought it toward his face, fascinated, wanting to see if his skin was as rough as it looked. Before my finger could touch him, he said, "Hey there girl, what are you doing?" and slapped my hand down.

Blushing horribly, I stuttered, "I'm sorry, it's just I have never see anyone as old as you. I'm sorry," I ducked my head, not knowing what else to say.

Off behind him, a voice called out. "Now I know you're getting old, Victor, slapping that pretty young girl's hand away. You come over here darling, you can touch anything you want." The voice quipped, causing the whole room to break out in laughter.

"You go letting pretty young girls touch you, Jackson, and Maureen is gonna be chasing you around the house with her frying pan," Victor snorted, causing another round of laughter.

"Now girl, you come sit with me, I'll be protecting you from those dirty old men." Peeking up through my lashes, I saw Johnathon smiling, motioning with his head for me to follow Victor. Turning to Tristian, I saw a small smile on his face and his hand went to my back, pushing me forward. Slowly following, I listened as he muttered, "As if those old dogs would know what to do with a young thing like her. Young enough to be their granddaughter she is. They'll be lucky if I don't make a round and be talking to their wives." He continued to mutter like this all the way to his seat. Dropping down to his chair with a groan, he waved his stick at the chair next to him. "Come on girl, sit down. You better not be expecting for me to stand and hold it out for you. If that's what you're waiting for, best look to those two boys."

Wide-eyed, I moved quickly to the seat and sat down, earning a smile from the crusty old man. Squinting at me, he said, "Now girl, best you explain yourself."

Staring at him, not knowing what to say, he shook his head at my silence. "Why did you try and poke me in the face?"

Shaking my head, I said, "No, no, I wasn't trying to poke you, I just wanted to see what your skin felt like. I've never seen someone as old as you and I wanted to know if it felt the same as mine." I fretted, my words tumbling out, horrified that he would think that I would try to hurt him.

Blinking at me, he looked at me like I was some strange creature. "What do you mean you've never seen someone as old as me?"

Pushing my hair behind my ear, I said, "The oldest person I've ever seen was in their forties, I've never seen someone as old as you before." I was embarrassed, as everyone seemed to be hanging on our every word.

If it was possible he looked at me even more strangely. Luckily, before Victor could ask me anything else, Johnathon spoke up. "She's telling the truth, Victor. Where she comes from, most people are put to death in their twenty-first year."

Total silence met with his announcement as every eye stared at me in shock. For long minutes not a sound was heard until Victor asked, "Where do you come from, girl?"

"We," I began, looking to Tristian, "come from the caverns below the city."

"We all came from the caverns at one point, child. Are you saying you live in the Stone City in the caverns? But that can't be right, they don't put people to death for turning twenty-one," he said worriedly, looking to Johnathon like he was afraid that they did.

"No, we come from the caverns ruled by the City to the West. We've been kept as their slaves since the great cleansing. Until we escaped, we thought that the land above the ground was destroyed and could no longer sustain life," I quickly said, wanting to calm him, but my words only seemed to make him more upset.

"I told you that those bastards were hiding something," he yelled, waving his stick at Johnathon, "but I never thought it be something as bad as this."

Grabbing the stick, Johnathon pulled it out of Victor's hand, and set it down. "Unfortunately, that's not the worst thing that they're doing to their people."

"What worst thing could they be doing to those people? They have them trapped down there, keeping them as slaves. Killing them when they reach twenty-one. What more could they be doing to those people?" he demanded loudly enough that I think they heard him outside. Looking to me, he grabbed my arm, "What more are they doing to your people, girl?"

Looking to Tristian as Victor shook me, I heard Tristian say, "Let her go now," barely containing his anger.

Shocked, Victor quickly released my arm before turning his attention to Tristian. "Well than boy, you had best be telling me what they are doing to your people," he growled, his voice just as mean as Tristian's.

Going down on his haunches until he was eye level with Victor, he said, "First, my name is not boy, it's Tristian. Second, her name is not girl, it's Misty. Now you want to know what they do to my people during their twenty-first year. Well, I'll tell you. They round us up for a lottery and we all have to journey to a place called the Cavern of Death. Once we're there, one hundred lottery winners are chosen who won't have to enter and are allowed to age though they rarely last into true old age. The unlucky ones who don't win are sent into the Cavern of

Death to die—or so we thought. What we learned before we escaped was at the beginning of our time within the caverns there was a disease that killed all the animals. Well, this put our government in a food-source shortage that they were able to rectify by saying that the Cavern of Death was a form of population control." Watching the old man's face as what Tristian was saying began to sink in, I put my hand on his arm, wanting to stop him. Shaking my hand off of his arm, he turned a hard look to me, telling me without words to remain silent before gluing his eyes back to Victor's. "Once we reached the surface and heard shots coming from the direction of the city, we figured that all are not used for food for the Loyalist, but some are taken as slaves to work for them as well. Now, old man, do you understand what they do to our people?" He hissed, before rising and stepping back.

Retching sounds and soft weeping could be heard in the aftermath of his speech. Even Johnathon, who already knew, looked green from Tristian's telling. Standing up, I moved into Tristian's side, letting my fingers graze his, the stiffness of his body telling me he would allow nothing else.

"They need sanctuary. There are many within the government, both theirs and ours, that will not want their truths to be known," Johnathon stated, looking at Victor's still dazed face.

"Yes," he weakly said before clearing his throat. In a stronger voice, he continued. "Yes, they can have sanctuary among us. Cullen, call a meeting of the council for tonight," he said, as, a man stepped from the shadows who I hadn't noticed before.

"Victor, Johnathon should get back, we don't want there to be any suspicion that he helped them escape," the shadow man said before leaving.

"He's right, Johnathon, go, we'll take care of these two," said Victor. Nodding his head, Johnathon turned and left without a word.

Focusing his attention back on us, Victor said, "Would you like to rest or"—stopping a moment taking a breath—"or would you like to eat?" he asked, looking nauseas at the words.

"I think it's best if we rest," Tristian answered, still tight with anger.

With a wave of his hand, a middle-aged woman stepped forward. "Karen give them a room upstairs so they can rest. I have a feeling that they'll need all that they can get," he said.

Following the woman through the room, I was careful to keep my gaze straight ahead, not wanting to see the looks the other people wore. The woman led us up through the stairs several floors before stopping and letting us into a large room. With a small bow of her head, she turned and left. Walking into the room I let my bags fall to the floor. Moving to the window, I stood to the side and looked out, everything seemed to be as it was when we arrived. There was no angry mob pointing to our window, screaming "monsters." Turning to look at Tristian, I saw that he was sitting on the bed with his head bowed into his hands, his anger still showing through the rigidness of his body.

Slipping off my shoes, I walked on silent feet until I was in front of him. Going to my knees, I sat in front of him, waiting patiently for him to acknowledge me. The tick of the clock sounded the minutes that passed and still he just sat there like stone. A darkness spread out from him that had never been there before. The past and every dark memory enveloped him. Leaning myself forward, I moved toward him, tentatively reaching out my hands. Like a snake, he struck, shackling my wrists, pulling me into him until our faces where inches apart. I didn't recognize the person that looked at me from the face I had known all my life, instead of my friend, something dangerous stared at me. Hard lips crashed into mine, dominating me as I was pulled tighter into his body. Releasing my wrists that were now pressed between our bodies, his hand dug into my hair, tilting my head to his will. Circling my throat with his free hand, he squeezed, causing me to gasp, giving him access to plunder my mouth.

In a single motion he lifted me up into his arms, never releasing my mouth as he turned and laid us across the bed, the weight of his body pressing me deep into the mattress. It seemed like hours had passed when he finally released my mouth. Taking his hands from my hair and neck, he framed my face as he stared down into it. Want, need, and pain raged through his eyes before he closed them and turned to his side, keeping me wrapped tightly in his arms as if he was afraid I would escape. The pounding of our hearts and harsh breathing were the only sounds in the room. A riot of feelings ached through my body. As I tried to free my hands, it only caused him to grip me tighter. Undeterred, I tilted my head up until my lips were at his throat. Darting my tongue out, I tasted the saltiness of his skin before placing light kisses. Shudders ran through his body. Trying again, I slowly moved my arms and this time he allowed it. Keeping my hands on his body, I made my way up until they framed his face. Leaning back so I could see his face, I watched a look of bliss pass over it as his eyes fluttered.

I had never touched a boy like this or been touched like this until Tristian. With feather strokes, I moved my fingertips over his face to his lips. With a gentle motion, I ran one finger over his lips, drawn in by the softness. Inching up, I let my lips replace my finger with barely-there kisses before wrapping him in my arms and pulling him atop me. In silence, that's how we laid, with his head upon my chest, as I stroked his hair and shoulders, feeling the tension slowly drain from him. I don't think he had truly slept since the lottery and he learned the truth. Pushing everything from my mind except the feel of his body, I closed my eyes and with his scent surrounding me I drifted off, joining him in sleep. In his embrace was the only place that kept the nightmares away.

Chapter 13

A week has passed since we have arrived in our haven. The meeting of the council was basically us telling them of our life and the history of our people below the ground. Hour after hour we spoke, answering their questions. The hall that they held this meeting in was packed full of the residents of the village weeping, retching, and angry—cries echoed in the hall as we spoke. At the end I thought they would send us from the village, condemning us as monsters no different than those who imprisoned us. I was shocked when the people of the village spoke on our behalf and those of our people wanting to protect us and help them.

We've learned that everything on the surface was not as it appeared and that as Johnathon had said their government had changed since they had begun to trade with the city and not for the better. A woman told us in tears that one of the things that the city sent in trade was meat and the shame she had in buying it almost broke my heart. Anger was like fire that spread with each telling, moving through village after village. Afraid of what their government might do, I went to Victor, but he told me that though it spread, it only did to the most loyal among them.

He confided that he knew of the spies in each city, town, and village, so he was making sure that only the most loyal knew the truth. He also told me that we were being searched for. That they have been searching for us since the moment we disappeared. Terrified that we were putting these people in danger, I spoke to him of leaving, but he wouldn't hear anything of the sort. He told us that what was to come had been long in coming and whether we were here or not would make no difference.

Leaving Tristian in a meeting with the council speaking of plans, I walked through the village toward the forest, needing time to myself. Since the night Tristian had kissed me, again he had all but avoided me, only coming to bed after I was asleep and leaving before I awoke, making sure we were never alone if he could help it. Unsure why he regretted it so much that he avoided me and unsure of my feelings, I left the meeting not wanting to sit there while he ignored me. Moving deep within the woods until I could no longer hear the sounds of the village, I wandered aimlessly until I came across a river that reminded me of the one that we have found the day we crawled from the caverns. Slipping off my shoes and clothing, I waded in the cool water, allowing it to wash away my thoughts until nothing remained.

I swam until the sun had begun to dip in the sky, turning the water cold. Climbing out, I sat on the bank, staring at the dark depths and letting the breeze dry me. Twilight had come when I heard the first shot, it echoed in the silence, scattering the birds. Looked in the direction of the village, I whispered, "Tristian," pulling on my clothing. Terror gave me strength as I raced back the way I had come from. The continued fire of the guns was now quiet except for an occasional burst. Slamming myself to the ground at the edge of the forest, I looked in horror at the sight before me. The field was soaked in red, lifeless bodies of men, woman and children littering it. Their unseeing eyes stared at me just as accusingly as Rose's and my sisters' did in my dreams. Large amounts of people were huddled together in groups as armed men searched house to house. Tensing, I saw two men drag Tristian from the council hall, hanging limply between them. Loading him in a vehicle, the rest of the soldiers waited until it was moving down the road before getting in their own vehicles and following.

I stayed frozen in my spot long after they had left to make sure they were really gone before taking the blood-soaked walk through the field into the devastation below. Smoke filled the air from the smoldering fires as weeping woman wailed over their loved ones. Children wandered through the streets calling to mothers who would never answer. Moving toward the council hall that remained untouched, I saw Victor on its steps staring at the destruction visited upon his people. I felt the eyes that found me rising up and leaving their dead to follow behind as I went to stand before Victor. Standing at the base of the steps, I met his eyes, awaiting what was to come. Tristian and I had brought this upon these people; each death that had fallen on this day was mine to bear. These people had took us in and they had a right to their vengeance.

Instead of the hate I deserved, relief flashed in his eyes as they met mine. "They didn't get you!"

"No, I was in the woods and by the time I made it back here, they were carrying Tristian out. I am prepared for my punishment," I said loudly and clearly, wanting all who heard to know that I knew this was my fault.

Instead of the rightful cries demanding vengeance, the woman who showed us to our room the first day walked toward me. Carrying her dead child, she moved up the steps until she stood directly in front of me. Red tear-soaked eyes pinned to me, she spoke in a loud, carrying voice. "Look at my child, dead by the soldiers' hands. Innocent in this world, her life worth nothing to them. Our ancestors rebelled to end such tyranny, yet here we stand surrounded by our dead as a government tries to hide its sins. They think what they have done has broken us." Squeezing the limp bundle in her arms tighter to her, her voice becoming harder. "But we are not broken, all they have done is to make us more determined to set right the injustices forced upon us. So as you dig the holes to lay these bodies in, I want you to take this night deep into your hearts as you bury your dead. Carry your rightful vengeance deep within as we spread the events of this night to every village, town, and city. Let all that you come across know of this night, let them know that if they don't stand with us this may one day be their wife, husband, or child. Look to this girl in front of me. The government that did this, this night, has murdered all those that she has ever cared for, yet they could not crush her. Against insurmountable odds, she escaped and survived." Breaking her blazing gaze from mine, she looked out to the crowd. "Tonight take the bravery of this girl within you. She was not a sheep to be led to the slaughter, but a lion who fought her way free. If we do not stand up now it will be us thrown into the darkness, us who are slaves and food to those who believe themselves our betters. Go now, bury your dead, help the injured, and prepare yourselves for the coming of a new dawn in which what our ancestors gave their life for is realized. The freedom of all our people below and above. War is upon us and though we may not have started it, it is we who shall stand in righteous victory at the end," she finished, to the roar of the crowd.

Turning to look out at the crowd, the hate that I deserved was not on their faces. In its place stood determination. Determination to avenge their loved ones. Moving away, they quietly went to gather their families and mourn their loss. Turning back to the woman, I saw that Victor now stood with her, his hand on the child's still head as tears poured unchecked down his cheeks. The little girl must have been his granddaughter. Stepping forward, not wanting to intrude on their grief, but seeing no one else move to them, I said quietly, "I'll help you bury her," needing to do something to help the guilt that coursed through me that I knew would never go away.

Not looking up at me, the woman nodded and our sad little party joined the others walking through their town toward the cemetery on its outskirts. After the night's events, I was afraid that the fence that surrounded it would have to be brought down to fit all of its new occupants. The sound of shovels striking the ground was loud in the silent night; even the insects that could usually be heard filling the darkness were silent. Hours later, when the last body was placed in the ground, a man stepped forward that they called a priest. They had explained religion to me, but it was still a new concept, since it was forbidden in the caverns. He prayed for the fallen, then began to say something else, something that brought me to the thoughts that I had tried to block: "Ye though I walk through the valley of the shadow of death…"

As he spoke, his words brought the Cavern of Death to me, its endless darkness stretched before me, but instead of the unknown the truth of what that darkness held stared back at me. Instead of the fear that I usually felt at its thoughts, a cold darkness began to move through me. The darkness stopped my tears, it hardened my heart, as a feeling of nothingness moved through me. I was finally alone; they had taken everything from me. My hope for a new life swept away with Tristian. Standing separately from the others, I looked on. They were a group together in their grief, together in there vengeance. I thought was alone, separated from all those I held dear by death, separated by those that knew my sorrow by the tons of earth below my feet.

Closing my eyes, I let the darkness surround me, seep into my very essence. I owed these people whether they saw it like that or not. I owed them for every life taken this night. I would not hide from my debt but embrace it, hold it deep within. It would give me strength for what I had to do. They would not take my life in payment, but they would have it anyway, just in a different form. No matter what I had to do or how long it took, I would help them, being whatever they needed until they got what they craved. Their cravings were my own and I would nurture them within me as a mother nurtures her babe within her womb. Vengeance, I am your instrument; do with me as you will.

Chapter 14

There was no sleep that night as I stood at my window watching the morning dawn. The night's devastation was even harsher in the light. Fires still smoldered all around, people walked aimlessly, as if unsure that last night had happened. The click of the door told me I was no longer alone.

"You're needed in the council chamber now," Karen said quietly. Turning to her, I looked at the woman whose child I helped bury and followed her without a word. Stepping out into the light, the smell of death clung to the very air. As we moved toward the council's domain those that had moved without purpose through the night spotted us, and it seemed to bring life back to their bleak eyes. No words were spoken as our group grew, each person we passed gathering with us until it seemed what was left of the town walked into the council's chamber with us.

Breaking away, I walked straight up to stand before the council. None of its members had been killed, but each lost members of his or her family in punishment for having dared to speak against their government and mine. Not waiting for them to speak, I commanded, "I need you to explain about Prey," the unsure girl of yesterday gone.

Startled, it was the Elder Gideon who found his voice first. "They are those that escaped the Hunters of the city and found their way to us before they could be captured or killed."

Nodding my head, I kept my voice firm. "We need to gather as many of the Prey that we can and interrogate them."

Sighing in sadness, Victor began, "Misty, I know that Tristian's loss is hard for you…"

Cutting him off, I said, "This has nothing to do with Tristian. Those that you call Prey knew about the caverns and never spoke out and we need to know why. We also need their information about the Loyalist city and how they were able to escape."

Murmurs moved through the crowd as they realized that I was right. Why were we the first to speak of the caverns when others had escaped the city long before us? "They are within the Stone City. They all live within the Stone City," Victor said slowly, as realization of what I said moved through the council.

"Do we know how many of your people were found or were we the only ones attacked?"

"We were the only ones attacked," Victor replied.

Hardening even further. "Then we were betrayed. Someone told them that Tristian and I were among you. The force that they sent was one to make a statement, not one to search. By your own words, we were the only ones attacked," I stated, sure of it.

Anger ripped through the crowd at my words. Slamming his hand on the table in front of him for silence, Victor said, "I agree there is a traitor among our groups." Turning to look out at the crowd, he growled in barely contained anger, "All communication with groups in other communities will be approved by the council until this traitor is found and brought before us." Turning back to me, he said, "You're right, the Prey is what we need. It's time that they were brought before us; they hold the answers we seek."

Moving and taking a seat, we began to plan on how to steal these people from the Stone City. If I was right, these people were threatened never to speak a word about what happened within the Loyalist City if they wanted to live. Then to be sure that they didn't grow a conscience, they were kept close so they could be watched. I'm sure that they had killed as many that they could, but some hadn't been wounded and they weren't able to say that they were unable to save them. As the plans were laid, I told them that I would be going to collect them. This was not very well accepted until I said the one thing that they couldn't dispute—I was one of them. If we were going to get them to cooperate and get them out to question them without them trying to turn us in, the best chance we would have is for them to know they weren't alone that one of them was among them.

For hours we debated on who to use in the other villages and in the Stone City we would need some of the people if we even had a small chance of this working. We would need Johnathon to get us into the Stone City and that could be a problem. He was suspected in our disappearance and though they couldn't prove it, he wasn't as trusted as he had been before. Finally it was agreed that chances would have to be taken and lives sacrificed if need be. The village that these people had called home all their lives was no longer safe and would have to be abandoned. It would be the first place after last night's events that would be searched when the disappearances were noted.

What I learned that day was even if we hadn't come along, a revolution was inevitable. For generations, a secret had been kept within this village. A secret of underground bunkers built deep within the forest to be used in the event that they were discovered. Last night as we buried the dead, the children and many of the woman had been sent there to keep them safe. The place was stocked and restocked with food every year in the event that if something like this happened they would want for nothing. They knew that soldiers would be back, hoping that they could capture me, waiting until I felt safe to return then they would. Yes, plans within plans were made as a small group was selected to join me on my suicide mission. Yes, a suicide mission is what it was, the chance of success so slim it was almost nonexistent, but the reward so great that it had to be done anyway.

It was late when the meeting was finished and everyone was sent back home to gather their belongings. Small groups would be sent out to join the others in the bunkers all through the night, while others walked through the town as a distraction in case the scouts missed any hidden soldiers lying in wait, watching. My group would also begin its journey in the darkness, moving through the woods to avoid detection. In the darkest part of the night we left with no light to guide our way. My life in the cavern was a blessing for this, as I saw better in the night than in the light. On silent feet we moved, never stopping, never faltering. It was well into the next day, miles from where we began before we felt safe enough to rest. Hidden in a crop of rocks, we rested while sentries who were posted around watched, waiting for their turn.

For days we moved like this, avoiding all signs of life in the villages we passed. It had been decided that we would go two days and nights on foot before approaching a contact in the village or town we were near by then. This way there would be no clear path to us, but it would be before the soldiers realized that our village had been abandoned. Once that was realized, they would do everything to find their missing citizens. On the second night, we sat on the outskirts of a large town watching, waiting. Soldiers milled through its streets, their presence unexpected but something that we had to risk. When the streets had quieted and the soldiers wandered to their barracks, we made our move. Staying to the shadows, we went house to house, then to the darkened allies, weaving our path, careful to remain unseen until we reached our destination. An ordinary home on an ordinary street lay before us. Michael, the leader of our group, whispered for us to remain hidden as he approached it. Moving into the light, he walked over as if he belonged and knocked on the door. When a young woman answered, he spoke with her briefly before going in.

Twenty minutes passed before he returned to the door, signaling for us to come. In ones and twos we crossed the street and made our way into the dark house, acting as if we belonged. We were waved to the back of the house as we entered and we went to a large room with a man behind a desk and the girl who answered the door beside it. Staying to the back of the group, the others crowding in front of me, they blocked any view of me.

As the last person entered, the older man spoke. "What does the cause require of me, Michael?" It was evident that they knew each other.

"We need a way to make it into the Town of Twin Rivers," he answered, taking the seat in front of the desk.

Shaking his head, the man said, "That's impossible, all the roads are being watched. Something is going on. In the last week the presence of the troops in this area has doubled, also soldiers from the City to the West have joined them. I might be able to get one, maybe two, of you through, but all six? No, we'd be caught for sure, I'm sure you understand."

"No, Finis, it is you who will understand. The cause requires you to get us all through, so a way must be found," Michael told him in an even voice as he leaned forward. "Two days past, our village was attacked by soldiers of the City to the West who knew of our visitors. They murdered indiscriminately men, woman, and children." Stopping to watch the other man's face before continuing, he said, "I don't care what it takes. What bribes you have to make or what lives have to be taken, you will get us to Twin Rivers tomorrow."

Tightening his face as the girl beside him gasped, he asked, pushing the words out "My daughter and her family?" This, I thought to myself, was why Michael chose to push on and make it to this man for help. No words were needed as he looked into Michael's face. "Take the rooms upstairs and I'll prepare everything. You'll leave at first light," he said, watching the girl as she raced from the room. Filing out of the room and up the stairs, I heard him speak out before Michael could close the door. "Is the traitor dead?"

Tightening his grip on the handle before answering, he said, "No."

"He will be," the man behind the desk murmured, loud enough to be heard before the click of the door silenced him.

Stopping at the top of the stairs, we waited for Michael to join us. Moving past us, he opened doors, putting us in rooms, two per room. Holding me back, he brought me to the last room, and giving me a gentle push, he told me to take the bed as he went to a sofa to the side. Exhausted, but unwilling to get into a clean bed this dirty, I went to the connecting bathroom to take a quick shower. Twenty minutes later, eyes drooping, I crawled into the bed careful not to wake Michael. Sleep and darkness took me as soon as my head hit the pillow.

It was dark, but it's always dark here. The cold of the caverns were settled so deep into my bones that they were a part of me. Walking through the streets, it was as if I had never left. Except they were empty, the cavern was empty. Running to my house, I threw open the doors, searching room to room, but no one was there. Racing through the cavern, I found myself at the doorway. The doorway to the Cavern of Death, its blackened abyss daring me to enter, to join the others. I was alone, but if stepped through I could join them once more. Peace came to me at the thought of being with them again and I fearlessly stepped in. As I entered the darkness, it gave way to light and sun, filled with laughing people grabbing my arms pulling me with them. To a table they pushed me, telling me to eat as platters were lifted. Empty eyes stared at me from posed bodies as each lid was lifted. One by one the members of my family and friends were revealed as they ate around me. At last there was only one left and with shaking hands I reached forth, lifting the huge lid, the lid that should have been heavy and bulky considering its size, but was light as air. Dropping it, it fell to the floor, causing them to laugh harder, raising forks full of food to my lips. Covering my mouth to block them, I couldn't run as my eyes stayed locked with Tristian's lifeless eyes as he joined my other accusers.

Hands gripped me hard, shaking me, forcing my eyes open. Biting back the scream I could feel in my throat, my unfocused eyes found Michael's concerned ones. Shaking as the breeze from the window touched my sweat-covered body, I tried to calm my pounding heart. Letting me go, he went and closed the window. I could feel his eyes upon me after he gazed out to make sure my screams had not alerted others to our presence.

"Please," I whispered, not even sure I knew what I was asking. Slowly, as if not to startle me, he moved back to the bed laying down beside me. Staring into his eyes we remained like that, not touching, until a dreamless sleep reclaimed me.

Chapter 15

Whispering voices woke me. Turning to the sound, I saw Michael and Garth, his second-in-command, at the door. Sitting up, they turned to me, Garth nodding his head before walking away. "We'll leave soon get ready, so meet us downstairs," Michael said, before following him. Grateful he wasn't making a big deal out of last night, I got up and got ready. Hurrying, I joined them as quickly as I could. I walked in just as breakfast was going on the table. Ignoring the look of concern I saw in the others' eyes as they looked up at me, I went and took the empty seat by the girl from last night. Luckily she was no more interest in speaking than I did, the grief that still ravaged her face from the night making that plain. Keeping my gaze to my plate, I listened as the others spoke of how we were going to be traveling. We wouldn't be able to go together and would be moved in two separate trucks. Rushing through breakfast, our host said it was time. Grabbing our bags, we spilt up into two vehicles and drove to a warehouse, where once the doors were closed behind us, we got out and were rushed to the awaiting trucks. Careful to remain unseen, we made our way to the back of the trucks, sliding into a secret compartment. No sooner had the door closed then we were on our way, forced to stand and remain quiet through the long journey.

We were stopped a total of five times, each scarier than the next. As the trucks were searched, the smallest of noises would mean our deaths. It was late into the night when we were finally let out, the truck having arrived and been unloaded hours before, we were forced to remain until all the workers had left for the day. The soft click of the latch being undone caused me to tense as the door was opened to reveal a child no more than twelve. With a finger to her lips she motioned for us to join her. Cramped, my body moved slowly as I exited the compartment, afraid that I was going to collapse without the walls to hold me up. With a scared look in her eyes, she waved at us to hurry as she looked around in fright. Unable to give in to my pain, I rushed to keep up with the others as we jumped from the truck and ran into the shadows that held the rest of our group.

Luckily we didn't have far to go or I wouldn't have made it. Around the side of a house, we were let into a darkened basement, the little girl gone—her job done. No one was there to meet us, though food had been laid out and beds littered the room. It was a safe house. No one spoke as we ate, some going to the shower, some to the beds as they finished. The self-imposed silence that began earlier today no one wished to break, as we were drained, needing time to themselves. Sitting down on a mattress near me, I propped myself up on the wall, my stiff body protesting, wondering what the next move was. I must have dozed off when a noise in the darkness woke me. Tensing, I looked around to the sleeping forms spread through the room, surprised to find Michael next to me. Lifting my head from his shoulder, I quietly made my way to the side of the door, a knife gripped firmly in my hand and waited––I didn't have long. A lone figure came through, closing the door behind. Waiting until he was in front of me, I struck. Slamming my body to his, I got us both to the floor, my knife flying unerringly to his heart. A hand lashed out, gripping my wrist, stopping its flight, and flipping us. I found myself trapped under the intruder, my knife useless.

The lights blinded me when they came on. So much so that when my vision came back to focus, we were surrounded by the others now awake and I was staring into a familiar face. Letting my knife fall from my useless hand and deciding to brazen my way out, I lifted my hips before going limp and gazed at my captor with a droll look "What have you been eating, bricks? Get up, Johnathon, my legs are falling asleep."

Smiling, he said, "It's good to see you, too, Misty." He stood up, pulling me with him. "Though I would have thought that this is the last place I would see you," he said, turning questioning eyes to Michael. The reprimand in his tone was clear.

Seeing the fight brewing, I snatched up my knife, putting it back before grabbing Johnathon's arm. "The council sent me, we agreed that my people would feel safer fleeing if they knew that there was one of their own among you."

Still unhappy, he turned back to me, surprising me when he pulled me into his arms. "I just glad you're OK," he said.

Before I could say anything, I was pulled from his arms over to Michael's side. With a dark scowl on his face, he growled, "Why wouldn't she be?"

A speculative look passed in Johnathon's eyes before a smile took its place. "Ah, Michael, I see you're as charming as ever. Come now, let's sit, there's much to discuss and little time."

When they just stood there posturing, I pulled my arm from Michael's firm grasp and went to the table, rolling my eyes. Shaking his head and giving a small laugh, Johnathon followed, Michael right behind. Ignoring them until everyone was settled, I asked the question that I knew could break me. "Do you know what they did with Tristian?"

A dark look passed over Johnathon's face before he answered me. "He was taken to the City to the West. Our government turned him over immediately to their representatives. They stated that you and Tristian were criminals, leaders of a terrorist organization whose lies were looking to undermine their government in a bid for power. They've denied everything, saying that it was propaganda by your organization in an attempt to gather an armed force of our people and seize control."

"They handed him over without proof?" I asked, knowing what he was going to say and hoping that I could still do what I came here to do after he answered.

"Their lies were corroborated by the escaped Prey from the city," he replied, confirming my fears. "You're wanted for treason and anyone caught harboring you will be put to death." Nodding my head, I was afraid that if I tried to speak my voice would betray the pain that I tried to hide. I guess a small part of me hoped that Tristian would be here and we could rescue him. That small piece of me that held hope was gone now, as dead as he surely was.

Michael's hand reached under the table, taking my cold one. "Will we be able to get to the Prey?"

Slowly shaking his head, Johnathon said, "It will be difficult, but not impossible. They are being watched more closely, but aren't under constant guard. You've actually arrived on the best day possible to grab a few of them. A large fair will start tomorrow and the servants will be there buying for the households they serve. Your problem, though, won't be grabbing them; it will be getting them out of the town. Once night falls, it will be noticed that they didn't return and a search will begin. Every house, every vehicle on the roads stopped and torn apart."

"I agree, which is why I think our best bet is the forests."

"The forests will be the last thing searched," Johnathon remarked, not agreeing or disagreeing.

"I know that it's not the best option and it will take the longest, but I think it is the only option that might work.

There are not many, especially in this area, who are comfortable in the forest. Most of the people are out just far enough to spot anyone making their way toward the town, no one is posted past the bridge," Michael reasoned.

"Agreed," Johnathon said, turning his gaze back to me, where he looked for a long moment before speaking again. "Will you be able to deal with these people knowing what they did?"

With dead eyes, I met Johnathon's gaze. "I know what I have to do, don't question me again," I told him harshly, angered at him for voicing my own thoughts aloud. Only the knowledge of what I could do with them after we got the information that was needed and they held no further use calmed me enough to remain at the table to hear the rest of the plan. Letting none of my thoughts show, I listened carefully, now more determined than ever to save as many of these people as I could so I could kill them later. Traitors against your own people were dealt with harshly among my people. Now I'm glad I never told the others or they would know that I would wait as long as necessary to enact my revenge. I would have to make sure that the Prey didn't realize that I knew what they did until it was too late or they would never come with us. Unlike these surface people, they would know that the death that I had planned for them would be more horrid than any death that the city would give them. I could forgive them for wanting a life, but not for taking Tristian's.

Moving away to gather my stuff to give to Johnathon, who would be hiding it all within the woods for us to collect later, I was so caught up in what I was doing I didn't hear Johnathon approach. "He was alive when he left," he said.

What did he think that would make me feel, better? "He's dead now, so it makes no difference," I replied, turning and handing him my bag before going back to the table to eat. Ignoring everyone, I sat there and slowly ate, nursing my hate deep where no one could see while bringing to the surface the face I would need to make the traitors trust me. Slowly the mask of the old Misty began to rise, the one that had cared for her sisters, no matter what they did. Once I was sure that it was firmly in place, I talked to the others around the table to judge its effect. Their smiles and laughter told me that it worked, only Johnathon and Michael looked at me strangely, not trusting it. Thankfully they weren't the ones I was looking to convince.

It was now light and Johnathon was long gone to take care of his mission. Changing into clothing to blend in, we went out and made our way to the fair. The images that Johnathon showed us of the Prey and our escape routes were burned into my mind. With a carefree, excited air we made our way through the streets, blending seamlessly with the others around us. The fair was amazing—sights, smells, colors surrounded us and the old Misty loved it. With smiles and giggles, she touched and tasted all that the vendors showed her, while the new Misty kept a sharp lookout for what she had come for.

We found the first one quickly after arriving, a timid, mousy woman moving through the crowd, her dark hair hanging over her face. Making my way toward her, I joined her, looking at fabrics—the conversation was one-sided until I finally lured her into feeling comfortable. Keeping up a steady chatter, I moved with her booth by booth as the men followed discreetly behind. After buying her a sweet treat, we laughed together. I got her to follow me down a side alley, saying that I knew of a vendor at the end. It wasn't until we reached the end and she saw there was no exit that she began to get nervous. Turning back, her fears were confirmed as the men blocked the only exit.

Defeat was heavy in her eyes when she looked at me. "Please make it quick," she said.

As if I would give her a quick death after what she did, but I knew that *that* Misty couldn't come out. Keeping my mask in place, I said, moving closer, "We're not here to hurt you, we're here to save you." Disbelief flashed in her eyes as she looked at me, glancing fearfully back at the others keeping their distance, trying not to frighten her more than she already was. Knowing that I had to hurry, I kept going, taking her hand to bring her attention back to me. "You know that if the Loyalist city had sent us for you, we wouldn't be speaking. These people are part of a resistance and they need your help. We need you to come with us so that we can save our people in the caverns and make sure that they can never again do what they have done to our people to the people on the surface." Thinking of my sisters to put feeling in my voice, I said, "We need to help them. When you escaped our government, you thought you would be free, but you're not. You're still their slave. Come with us, help us, and be truly free."

"You're from the caverns?" she whispered.

Smiling with tears in my eyes, I said, "Yes, will you come with us and take a chance to truly be free and help free those still trapped below?"

Hope shone in her eyes as if I was her salvation. "What do I have to do?"

Got her. Waving the men toward us, they quickly told her what to do. To remain as she was, shopping until it was time to leave, while we searched for others. She quickly told us that she could help us. She knew where the others would be and she would help us gather them. It was better than we could hope for. With her help, what would have taken most of the day only took a few hours. Knowing which to approach and which were too broken to help, we gathered a total of twelve, more than we dared believe that we could. It wasn't even noon yet when we made our way into the forest. No one spoke as we avoided the sentries and raced for the bridge. I couldn't believe how close we were to it—what had taken Tristian and I days took only hours with the path Michael lead us on. That is where our problem would come from—there was no way of crossing the river without being seen.

Finding our supplies, we were told to stay as Michael broke away from us. Changing into the clothing left for us, we waited for Michael. Returning fifteen minutes later and motioning for us to cross, the blood on his knife told the story. Quickly we moved, terror giving us speed as the sun sank lower into the sky. Tired and winded, no one complained or asked for a break, and when the weaker ones fell, others gathered them up, pulling them along. The sun had long ago set and night was deep upon us when Michael found a spot where he said we could rest. Falling to the ground, the Prey laid there as we handed out food and water, forcing them to partake before an exhausted sleep took them. No fire was lit that night; it was warm enough that it wasn't worth the risk for a hot meal. Going to the men, I told them that I would take the first watch, the look on my face stopping them from arguing. For hours I looked out into the night, ignoring my thoughts until it was time to wake the next watch. After I was sure that he would stay awake, I went to where Michael lay and quietly put my back to his, careful not to touch, letting my exhausted body claim the sleep it needed.

The sun was just touching the sky when I was shaken awake. Feeling as if I hadn't slept a wink, I rose without complaint, knowing sleep was a luxury that we couldn't afford. Coming to sit next to me, Michael brought me food and water, and silently we sat eating our meager meal. A shadow fell upon me, causing me to look up at the first woman we found. Hesitantly she sat in front of me. Others, seeing her approach me, became bolder and moved to sit behind her. "My name is Tara," she said, holding her hand out to me.

Staring at it a moment, I swallowed my bile before reaching out and taking it. "I'm Misty."

"We"—she started, waving to the group behind her—"wanted to thank you for taking us from there. I don't know how much longer they were going to let us live."

Pretending that I had no idea, I asked, "What changed?"

Sadness and shame washed through her face before she lowered it to look at the ground. "It was just becoming too dangerous to allow us to live."

LIAR! I wanted to scream as she sat there, but I held it back, instead saying, "This may not be much of a better chance, but at least it will be a chance." Standing up, I made a show of gathering my stuff, trying to ignore them as they smiled at me in gratitude. Finally unable to take it anymore, I said, "We'll be leaving soon, why don't you all go and help the others pack." Nodding their heads like children, they stood and scurried away.

Mumbling to Michael that I'd be right back, I rushed into the woods, needing a moment to collect myself. Going as far as I dared, I slammed my hands into a tree, leaning in. I let my head hang down as I tried to reign in the darkness coursing through me. I knew that no matter how much I wanted to, I couldn't act on those feelings yet, I had a debt to pay to the lifeless bodies in the field. What was owed to me would have to wait.

I was so wrapped up in the noises buzzing through my head that I didn't hear Michael's approach. "The life that you and those people have been forced to live is one that I can never imagine," he said as he moved behind me. "Each one of you have a common core of pain before it branches out and your individual pain starts." Reaching out and gathering me into his arms, he pulled me back until our bodies were flush and his lips were to my ears. "At that point, you don't know their suffering any more than they know yours." Touching his lips to the shell of my ear, he said, "You would have died for your loved ones. You would kill for your loved ones. These people lived in spite of their loved ones. Blocking the truth out so they could find the courage to face the next day. There are many forms of courage, but sometimes surviving when there is nothing left to live for is its own form of courage." Releasing me, he stepped back and turned, walking away. "It's time to leave."

Turning, I followed him, staring unseeing at his back as the true meaning of his words swished around in my head. He knew. He knew that I but bided my time waiting. Pushing the thoughts away as we made it back to camp, I collected my bag and silently followed for another grueling trek through the woods. For three days we kept up the pace until what we feared would happen did. It was midafternoon when we heard the air vehicle moving our way. Scattering, we hid as it passed over us, searching. We stayed hidden like that for well over an hour before we dared to move. After that, it was decided that moving during the day had become too much of a risk. We found a place to make camp that hid us from view both around and above. Doubling the watch, we gathered to pore over the map, trying to find the safest way to approach the village. It would take us another four days moving in the dark rather than the two that it would have been if we could still move during the light. Silence was the key if we wanted to make it there alive. We were sure that they were moving in from the other direction, trying to find us and those that fled, leaving the village empty. It would be a close call to make the place that we marked to make camp before the sun rose, but it was a risk that we would have to take. Joining the others who were already asleep I laid down until the darkness came.

The soldiers were everywhere during the day; we listened as they thrashed through the woods, moving too close for comfort at times to our hiding spot. We were on the last night of our journey and discovery was more of a reality than ever. Guns and knives clutched in our hands at all times, sleep was impossible a small doze all that most of us were able to get. The bunker was a day's journey from the village and with how close we were, we figured that the soldiers must have set their base of operations within the village itself. Our only saving grace was that they didn't search in the night. We were right not to move during the day; if we had, we would have been caught long ago. Darkness was approaching; the day's light moved down the small cave's wall that we were crammed into, basically sitting on top of one another. We could hear the soldiers coming back in our direction to make their way back to camp. As they moved past, we all gave a sigh of relief thinking ourselves safe from discovery.

It was well into the dark when we left our little hideaway. Moving silently, we hurried as quickly as we dared, careful not to make a sound. The ones at the rear of our party disguised our trail as we pushed forward. It was close to dawn when we heard something that made my heart stop. A twig snapped and voices grumbled in the dark as two soldiers stepped right into our path, not five feet from me. Instinct to survive rushed through me as the soldier closest to me opened his mouth, I lunged, fear giving me strength and surprise the advantage—I brought us to the ground, driving my knife deep into his throat. With dispassionate eyes, I watched as life left his. Uncaring that I had just taken a life, it was but the first of many I was sure I would have to take in this new world. The part of me that would have cared was long since buried deep within me. Unfortunately, the others weren't as quick. The sound of a gunshot echoed around us the other soldier got off a round before they were able to silence him. We were out of time, stealth was no longer an option, they were coming, and if we did not reach the bunker before they found us, we never would.

Racing, we heard their approach moving quicker than I would have thought possible; they made their way unerringly in our direction. Our capture would have been assured if two member of our party had not moved away from us, racing in another direction. The sound of their firing guns echoed in the distance, drawing the soldiers to them. Dawn had come, the entrance to our haven stood before us, risen from the ground as its keepers waved at us to hurry. Grabbing my arm, Michael pulled me forward. He and I were the last to enter as the lift descended into the ground, hiding us from those that would see us dead. Two lonely shots sounded, echoing through the forest. Their sound as clear as a bell for those who understood the soldiers would not capture any of us this day.

Chapter 16

Twenty-four hours had passed since we arrived. The council had given us this long to recover before calling us to them, unable and unwilling to wait any longer. My sleep was plagued with nightmares as I slept alone in my room. Standing before the mirror, I threw cold water on my face, wiping the remnants of what little sleep I had gotten from it. Going to the door when the knock sounded through the empty room, I opened it and followed the man on the other side to the meeting hall in the center of the complex. The halls themselves were crowded with people the closer we came, overflowing from the meeting hall that was unable to hold them all. Parting for us, they whispered as we passed, touching my arm and smiling as if they were happy that I returned to them alive. Entering the hall, the crowd parted to let us pass, allowing us clear access to the front before moving back, closing the path behind me.

Seated high up, the council waited, watching me. Bowing my head to them, I went to where Michael and the others of our group were seated and took the empty seat next to him.

Looking out into the crowd, the Councilman Samson said, "We call this meeting of the council to order." The silence was instantaneous. No one wanted to miss a word of what was to come. "We are pleased to see that so many of those who accepted the mission have made it back to us and grieve with the families of those who did not. Their sacrifice will not be forgotten." Turning to look at Michael, Councilman Samson said, "Commander, the council has some questions for you that we will speak of later. For now though, we need to speak with the fruit of your mission—those you brought back with you."

Standing, Michael motioned the first woman we found to step forward, looking back at the council. "This is Tara," he said, as the terrified woman stepped forward. "She was instrumental in helping us gather the others quickly," he said, stepping back, motioning her forward.

Smiling kindly at the frightened woman, the council said, "Child, you have nothing to fear from us, we will not harm you. We have brought you and the others here to answer questions no one else has the answers to anymore. We will not judge you on anything you say, so please be honest with us." At her timid nod, he continued, "How long ago did you escape the city?"

"Four years ago," she whispered.

"Louder, please, my dear, some of us aren't as young as we used to be and our hearing is not as it once was."

In a louder voice, she said, "Four years ago, sir."

Nodding his head approvingly, he said, "And how did you escape the city?"

Looking with wide eyes back at the other Prey before she caught herself and turned quickly back to answer the floor in front of her, she said, "We didn't escape the city."

Murmurs moved through the crowd, so the councilman raised his hand to silence them "Then how did you get to Twin Rivers?"

"We are Prey, sir," she said, as if that made all the sense in the world.

Seeing that this was going to take forever with this line of questioning, I stood. "Victor, members of the council, may I ask her a few questions?"

After some quiet words among them, they told me to proceed, and I turned to Tara. "Look at me," I said harshly, forcing her to raise her frightened eyes to mine. "What is Prey?"

Seeming to be able to function better with my harshness, like any good slave, she stood a little straighter as she began to speak. "Prey are those that have displeased their masters or are too old to be of use and are let loose from the city to be hunted by the Hunters for sport."

Seeing me smiling my approval at her words, she seemed to relax a little. "So you and the others escaped the Hunters?" I asked.

"Yes, we escaped and the townspeople found us and took us in."

"Why did you not tell them about the City to the West, or what they had done to you?"

"At first we were afraid that they would give us back, then later, when we realized that they weren't like those that we escaped, others came to see us. They said that if we ever told anyone about what goes on at the city, we would be returned there."

"Were you born above ground or below it?"

"I was born below, but there are many born above also that serve the masters."

"Loyalists!" I spit out, uncaring that I was scaring her enough to step back. "They are not your masters, they are Loyalist scum and you, being born in the caverns, should know that." Her cowardness at those words, even when she was safe, was too much for me to bear. Realizing that my mask was slipping, I worked it back in place. "Forgive me, Tara," I continued, at her uncertain nod, "How did they take you from the caverns?"

Still afraid to meet me eye, she said, "At the lottery. We entered the Cavern of Death—it was dark, so dark. We stood in silence, waiting when a bright light came on blinding us. High above, they stood looking down at us. Soldiers moved through the crowd, pulling those of us out that the ones above pointed to. Gathering us, they herded us to a room to the side and sealed us in. I can still hear the screams of those that were left in there, even through the thick wall we heard, as the soldiers standing with us laughed at the fear that it caused within us. A few moments after the last shrieks echoed and died, the door was opened and we were pushed back in with them. The ground was littered with their dead bodies. However they were killed was beyond painful, as those last moments were etched into their now-frozen faces. A single man now stood above, looking down at us and told us that if we did not do as we were told that what happened to them would be mercy compared to our fate. Leaving us without another word, the doors on the other side of the cavern opened, showing us the truth of the Cavern of Death"—Tara stopped, and looked around wild-eyed as if she was seeing the images again—"We were forced to drag the bodies out and clean the room, so many bodies, the smell causing us to retch and gag. When we were finished, we were taken by transport in a closed truck to the surface. My first look at the world above burned my eyes, but kicking us forward, the soldiers laughed at our pain. We were brought to a building. For weeks we stayed there as we were cleaned and our new duties explained to us through beatings and pain. One by one, we were brought to a block in the large courtyard in front of the building as the Loyalists examined us before we were sold to a new form of hell."

"Tell them Tara, say it. Tell them what the Cavern of Death truly is," I whispered so low that only she could hear me.

Tears poured from her eyes, unseeing. "It is a place of evil. I remember the hooks that the bodies hung from, waving there, waiting for their next victims. They made us watch. The smell as the skin is removed burns your nose. They made us watch our friends be slowly chopped and ground as a taster sat to the side and checked the quality, offering us some." Turning back to the others, she asked, in a little-girl voice, broken as the truth of her sins came to light, "Why didn't we tell? Why didn't we try and help them?"

Stepping back, I went to go to my seat when her voice stopped me. "Do you think we don't know who you are?" Stiffly, I turned around and faced her. "We came anyway because we know that what was done cannot be undone and we must be punished for it." A look of steel moved into her face, gone was the broken woman and in its place stood what she must have once been. "He didn't say a word as we lied and in our fear said the words we were trained to say. He just looked at us in understanding, not condemning us as he should have. I knew that as soon as you said that you were from the caverns who you were. We will do all to help these people and hopefully help what is left of our people and families below."

Letting my mask fall, I looked her in the eyes. "Do you think that will change what you have done?"

Shaking her head, she said, "No, what we have done cannot be undone and we accept what you will do. In truth, I think I will welcome it. At least it will silence the screams." She moved past me as another stepped forward to take her place.

The gallery was silent at our words. Taking my seat, I ignored the council's looks and was saved from speaking as the next one we saved began to tell what he knew of the layout of the city. Hour after hour passed before we left the Meeting Hall, the last speaker's words some of the harshest. They would be divided into groups to work with those to help build models and maps as we began our preparations for what was to come. Alone in my room, I stared into nothing, turned my head, and saw Victor walk into the room. Had he knocked, I wasn't sure, but there he stood.

Taking the seat across from mine, he stared at me as I spoke. "The maps aren't going to be enough. It's been a long time since they were held within the city and there is no telling how it has changed."

Sighing, he replied, running a tired hand over his face, "You're right, the council and our commanders spent the last hour discussing it. A reconnaissance mission is needed to check the city's defenses. We also have to find how high the corruption goes in our own government."

"They're going to be watching every town, city, and village closely. If news of your town's disappearance spread, it could start people asking questions the governments will kill to not answer," I murmured, my mind already moving to the trip that I was going to have to take. There was no way that I wasn't going to join the recon mission to the Loyalist city.

"We've made sure that only the most trusted know of it, so that it can be kept quiet as they gather others to the cause."

An un-humorous laugh escaped me, "Are they the same trusted souls that knew about me and Tristian?" I asked, angrily wiping a hand across my face. "I'm sorry, that was uncalled for. When are we going to be heading into the Loyalist city?"

"I don't think it would be a good idea for you to go in your current state," he said slowly.

Pinning him with my eyes, I pointedly said, "It's probably a better idea than me staying here, blood has a tendency to stain concrete," not hiding what I had planned after Tara's little speech.

Not bothering to pretend he didn't get my meaning, he replied, "We're trying to work out a plan now. It will be difficult with the patrols in the area."

"Maybe not," I smirked, leaning forward. "Maybe we're looking at this all wrong. Maybe we should just drive right up and go in through the front gate." The look he gave me told me he thought I had lost my mind, but with a small but true laugh, I said, "No, I'm not crazy. What I'm thinking is that the soldiers just drive right into the city. I mean, who is going to stop them?"

Looking at me in wonder as my plan sunk in, he started to laugh. "No, I don't suppose that they would search their own soldiers, now would they?"

"I don't suppose that you've managed to get your hands on any soldiers' uniforms through the years?"

Smiling at me like the Cheshire cat, he said, "Of our troops', absolutely; of the City to the West's soldiers, no"–

–he chuckled as my face dropped a little—"but we've managed to make very nice copies of them."

Leaning back against the wall, I said, "I think we'll need small teams infiltrating both side immediately."

"Agreed."

Hating what I was about to say, but knowing that it was needed, I added, "I also think we will need to take one or two of your refugees with us. They'll know the city and the people and without them we'll have no chance of finding allies within."

"I was wondering when that would cross your mind," he said, with a knowing look.

"I can't help how I feel about them, but this isn't about me, it's about your people and mine. I would rather see the living see justice and freedom than the dead who can no longer be harmed get revenge," I pushed out, hating every word because I knew it was true. I knew that Tristian would rather me help these people than be avenged.

"Our people," he firmly stated.

"What?" I asked, confused, tilting my head as I looked at him.

"They aren't *your* people or *my* people, they are our people. Below or above, we are one people."

Nodding my head, I said, "Well our people are in danger. We need to find who betrayed us if we are going to start gathering others to join. I don't know about you, but I don't plan on giving the city enough warning to prepare weapons that will send us back into those caverns for another few thousand years." Rising up from the bed, I held my hand out to help him up.

Gripping it tightly, he pulled himself up and looked me in the eye. "Agreed."

Walking out the door arm in arm to begin our strategy, I could only think one thing. We would never again surrender. Win or lose, there would only be one of us left standing when the smoke cleared. Death was coming on swift wings; it would be up to fate to decide who was carried away.

Chapter 17

The transport was right in front of us, but so were ten soldiers. Silently we waited for them to separate and move through the forest. We had been watching for days to see how each unit operated. While the local government's troops seemed to know everyone and interact, the city's soldiers were the exact opposite, staying within their own unit and almost hostile to the others. Which would definitely work to our advantage. This unit would leave tonight and return to the city for a week to gather supplies; it would be the perfect cover.

The council had made many decisions over the last week as reports had come in of attacks in other villages and towns as they searched for us and people were tortured for information about us. The unease that both governments had tried to silence only grew at their own actions of trying to capture me. The local governments' allowance of the Loyalist city's soldiers marching into their territory unchecked was only fueling our cause. The ones that had not wanted to get involved were now the most vocal calling for change. Refugees had been coming in from all over, quietly snuck into our bunker when the risk to their safety had become too great. So many had escaped that curfews had been put in many of these areas, promising death to any caught out during it.

A movement in front of me stopped my musing as I finally saw the soldiers break apart into groups of two and begin moving. Gripping my knife tighter behind my back, I waited for one to approach, as we were spread out though the forest like this. Leaning against the tree, I ignored the harsh question that the soldier barked, asking why I was in their sector. Dressed as I was in their uniform, I was a disobedient soldier, but not a threat. So focused were the two on me, they didn't see the two that stepped out behind them. It was quick and silent. One moment they were alive the next they weren't. Wrapping their wounds so a blood trail wasn't left, we moved the bodies to the hole dug the night before. Stripping them of their weapons and anything else of value that we might need, we threw them in and waited. Over the next hour, groups of two were brought to join them until all ten were accounted for. Burying them, we carefully hid the shovels, making sure no sign of what happened here was visible, and went to the awaiting transport.

Before anyone got in, we were each checked thoroughly to make sure that our uniforms were correct and that we put on our helmets. The ones that I expected to be the most nervous at this point were Tara and Samuel, the two Prey who volunteered to go with us, but they were rock-steady climbing in and taking a seat. I may not like them, but I couldn't help but admire the willingness to go back even knowing what would happen if they were discovered. Once everyone was seated and strapped in, we pulled out onto the main road to a checkpoint. They didn't even bother to say anything to us, just waved us by. I was right, this would be the best way to reach the city and have a chance of ever leaving it.

For two days we drove deeper into the enemy's territory. The closer we came to the city, the more often the checkpoints came, watchtowers hidden into forests between them. Seeing this, I couldn't help but turn to Tara and ask, "How did you escape?"

Smiling at me grimly, she explained. "I ran and ran until I thought my heart would burst, day and night, but the dogs still found my scent. I knew what they would do when they found me, so when I came to a cliff and saw the water below, I didn't hesitate to jump. What should have killed me was what saved my life. I don't know how far I was swept down, but when I used the last of my strength to pull myself out, I couldn't hear the dogs any longer. As I laid there, waiting to die, I realized something—that I had been dead for years and at this moment when death was closer to me than ever, I wanted life. So I pulled myself up and started walking. I collapsed at the bridge by Twin Rivers and when they found me I thought that I was done for, but they picked me up and cared for me instead." She turned to look out the window, silently telling me that she no longer wished to discuss it.

Staring at her for a moment, I let my eyes drift to the window next to her. "My cousin Rose was a Secretary," I started, not sure why I was speaking. "I was ashamed of her right up until the day of her lottery and I learned the truth, that she was actually a spy for the Elders. She discovered a map and vid disc that told the truth of the Cavern of Death and the caverns themselves. Instead of giving them to the Elders, she gave them to me, wanting me to save my sisters and myself. I don't know if you realize this, but there are hundreds of caverns below, filled with hundreds of thousands of our people." By their sharp indrawn breaths, I knew that they hadn't known. "I knew that I needed help to get my sisters to safety, so I showed my best friend Tristian and his father, an Elder, the truth. I couldn't leave Tristian behind to the death they had planned for him, and I couldn't leave without someone knowing the truth. One of my sisters betrayed us, telling her boyfriend, who was a traitor, though she honestly hadn't known that. She just wanted to take him with us. Freedom was closer than you could imagine when a cave-in took their lives and the lives of the soldiers who followed us. I think I would have laid there and joined them in death had Tristan not been there. The funny thing is, I didn't get up because he forced me to. I got up because of the debt I owed his family that I could never repay. By my sisters' actions she had condemned his father to death and the only thing I could give him in repayment was the life of his son," I finished, going silent as I watched the scenery. I don't know why I told them that, it was almost like I was explaining the reason that I would have to kill them. It wasn't because I couldn't understand what they did to live, hadn't I defended them to Tristian? No, it was because this was the only way I could repay my debt to his family ever. I knew that there was another reason that I didn't even want to admit to myself, because it no longer mattered, it would never matter again now that he was dead.

Lost in old thoughts and heartache, I was pulled back at my first sight of the Loyalist city. It was massive. Unlike the Stone city, it was built in the shadow of a large mountain, not inside the mountain. Monstrous buildings shot up past the great wall that encircled it, keeping all those within trapped. If I didn't know the evil that lurked within it, I would have said that it was magical in its beauty. Instead all I saw was the sinister shadow that the mountain cast upon it in the waning light. Michael hurriedly went over our procedure again, drilling into us to remain quiet unless spoken to. Motioning to Tara to join him in the front because of her familiarity with the soldier's ways, as she was forced to serve them at one time. A massive stone bridge lay before us that we would have to cross before entering through a set of steel gates that looked so eerily familiar, the final checkpoint. As still as statues we sat as a soldier approached, but instead of going to the window to speak with Michael, he moved to the front of the truck and scanned it.

After a moment of staring at his tool, he came to the side "You have three days. You're assigned to section R6 for your sleeping quarters. Have the truck brought to gate F4 to be restocked with the supplies and fuel." Without another word, he waved us past and turned, going back to his post.

Moving forward, Tara directed Michael to the correct gate. Soldiers were everywhere, supervising the workers of this area with vicious means. As she explained to us that this was the food intake and distribution center, we watched the half-starved wretches being beaten into the ground for not moving fast enough. The horror on the others' faces told me that they had never seen the likes of this before, but three of us just stared on sadly, knowing that this was life. Seeing their looks worried me, so I growled for them to "drop their face masks"—this wasn't the worst that they would see and if we wanted to make it out of here alive they would have to ignore it. Going to the spot that we were told to, we gathered our bags and exited the vehicle.

Following Tara without looking like it, we went to a passenger transport that traveled through the city. Taking an empty car, we silently waited as she punched our destination in. The thing moved so quickly and silently it felt as if you hadn't moved at all, but within moments we arrived to our sleeping area. Following the signs, we found the correct building and floor that led to a barracks that we appeared to have to ourselves.

Seeing our looks, Tara quietly told us, "The units stay by themselves, the government doesn't want fraternization between other units in fear of a coop. There are servants that clean the units and bring food to keep the pantries stocked, but no other soldier will enter."

Figures, the paranoid bastards. Wasn't that the reason that they kept the caverns separate? "Is it safe to speak?" I asked, looking around.

"Yes, its fine, they only bug the higher-ranking soldiers quarters with video and audio devices." she said, as if this was the most normal thing.

"So what's the plan? Are we going to go into the inner city now or later?" I asked, looking at Michael.

Eying Tara and Samuel, he said, "I'd like to get a feel for the place now, if you don't think it's too late."

Looking to each other, Samuel answered first. "No, we can still move around the city easily and do recon. This place is alive almost twenty-four hours a day for its citizens and soldiers."

"Should we change?"

"We should put on clean uniforms." Walking to a closet, he opened it. "The only time you will have to take your helmet off is if you enter one of the soldiers' eating and drinking establishments, otherwise no one will think anything of us leaving them on at all times."

Reaching in, I pulled out a uniform and going to the bathroom to change, I ignored the others' smiles at me as they just stripped where they stood. Waiting several minutes after I changed, not wanting to walk in on one of them half-clothed, I rejoined them. Ready, we moved to the door following Tara and Samuel as they led us back to the transport, punching in our location. They made us watch how it was done in case we were separated. The journey, like the one before, was quick, except this time when we stopped it wasn't to rows of bleak buildings, but a magnificent square. Bright lights and screens filled the area as images raced before us. Thousands of people moved around, rich Loyalists dressed in bright, expensive clothes were followed by their drab servants. Soldiers milled freely through the square, making it easy for us to blend in. The difference of the classes was visible in every move that each took. It was as if separate worlds existed in the same place. Following the others, we stayed as close as we could together without being suspicious, eventually splitting into two groups, one with Samuel and the other with Tara. Murmuring as low as they could, they explained each area we visited in the town, which was separated into five sections. The soldiers were on the outer area, where we were staying. Then came the government officials, the rich, the Loyalists, and the last owned slaves. Those slaves maintained the city works and whatever else that was required.

Moving along the side streets, we made our way to the slave section. Even if they hadn't told us, it would have been obvious that the closer we got the more run-down it became, nothing like the area we just came from. Even the soldiers' area, for how bleak it was, was one hundred times better than this. The screams of the women could be heard as we entered the area. Looking to Tara and Samuel, they understood what I was trying to say as they pushed to the front with me, keeping the others back before they did something stupid. The streets reminded me of home—they were dirty and fires burned in them as small groups of people milled around. Soldiers came out of houses we passed and the low moans of their victims could be heard before the doors shut. Keeping a careful eye on the others, I kept a blank face as we passed servants and soldiers. These people were broken, beaten so low I wasn't sure they could rise up enough to be of any help to us.

Worried at the vibe that I could feel moving through the others, I asked, "Tara, is there anyone that you or Samuel can think of to speak to in this area that could be of help to us?"

Not bothering to look at Samuel, she said, "I know of someone if he's still alive. This way." She led the way through the dark alleys as residents scuttled away from us like bugs. When she finally stopped, we were in front of a home that looked like any other. Raising her fist, she rapped on the door and we waited. Long moments passed before we heard the locks being disengaged and the door pulled open.

Absolute loathing flashed in the face of the man who opened the door before he quickly ducked his eyes. "Sirs, how may I be of assistance?"

Stepping forward, Tara pushed the large man back, the tension in is body telling us that he didn't want to let us in, but knew that he didn't have a choice. With his head still bowed, he stepped to the side, the tension in is body the only thing that betrayed his resistance. Going past him, we entered, gathering in what must be the living room and waited for the last to enter and the door to close.

"Is there any other in the house?" Tara asked, her voice sounding low and scratchy, as if she was disguising it.

"No, sir," he blandly replied. He was lying. I had done it enough that I could spot it.

"Is there any other in the house?" Tara demanded. "Or should we search?"

"My daughter, sir, is asleep but no one else," he reluctantly said.

"Where's the child's mother?"

This time he couldn't disguise the loathing he felt as he spit out one word: "Dead."

Tara took off her helmet. She had her eyes pinned on the bowed head, raising her hand, she touched the man's downturned face, causing his to flinch. "Dead, Tehenis, no. I may have been, but at this moment, I feel very alive, my love," she whispered, causing the man's head to jerk up. He stepped back, staring at her like she was a ghost.

Tears ran freely down her face as he reached a tentative hand out and cupped her cheek. Raising her own hand, she captured his and turned her face so her lips pressed into his palm. As if her touch had broken the spell, he reached out and pulled her to him. Wrapping her into his arms, he pulled them both to their knees, his legs unable to support him any longer. Heart-wrenching sobs poured from her as he stoically absorbed them into his own body, expelling ragged breaths. Gripping her hair tightly, he pulled her back to gaze down at her, disbelief clear in his eyes, as if he expected to wake at any moment to empty arms. "How?" he asked.

With a dazzling smile that showed the woman she must have once been, she said, "Oh, my love." It was all that she was able to get out before gripping his face and pulling it into hers, locking her lips to his. Not wanting to stare, I turned, trying to give them some privacy when a small girl of about seven walked sleepy-eyed from the other room. Looking around for the noise that woke her, she spotted me and her eyes filled with terror. Not wanting to scare her more than she was, I stepped back, trying to look nonthreatening. "Tara," I said, just loud enough to get her attention, causing the little girl to pull her frightened eyes from me and seek her father.

Neither of the two, still locked in one another's arms, heard me, but when the little girl whimpered "Daddy," the two flew apart, turning to look at her. Tara seemed to be the first to recover, trying to get to her feet and her daughter. Moving in front of her, I said one of the cruelest things I could ever have said. "No," turning to her husband, I said, "Put your child to bed so we can speak." Seeing that they were both about to argue, I went on, "A child is a special thing and at times does not know when or how to not tell the truth." Understanding dawned in her eyes as she bowed her head and whispered to her husband to put the girl to bed.

Swiftly rising to his feet, he went to his daughter, gathering her into his arms and taking her out of the room. Looking down at Tara's bowed head, I said, "I'm sorry," before going to check out the window to hide from the conflicting feelings that I was having. We all stayed silent as we waited for the man to return. It took him almost twenty minutes to return, but when he did, he assured us that she was asleep as he rushed back to Tara's arms.

Sitting down around the room, we gave the two of them as long as we dared. "Tara, we need to speak," I said, turning my eyes from her happy ones. Waiting until the two of them joined us, I said, "Tara, we don't have much time"

Nodding her head in understanding, she explained. "This is my husband Tehenis. He will be able to help us. He is the head servant of this section and will know everything we need to know about the city infrastructure and defenses."

"I'm sorry," he interrupted, "but who are these people? You're obviously not soldiers."

"No, my love, you're wrong—they are soldiers, but they are soldiers of the resistance." Pointing to me she said, "That is Misty, she escaped the caverns"—then sweeping her hands to the others—"and they are from the outlands where the other city lies."

Looking at me in wonder, he said, "No one's ever escaped the caverns—that's impossible!"

Smiling at him grimly, I said, "No, it's not. Two of us managed to get out, but I'm the only one left. The other was capture and killed, but not before we were able to spread the truth of the caverns and the government to the people who walk above." Turning and motioning to Michael, I said, "This is Michael, the commander of our unit. His people are slowly being overrun with Loyalists to our government and they have agreed to help us."

"I don't understand, what have they agreed to help us with?"

Staring at him a long moment, I said, "They've agreed to help us fight for our freedom and the freedom of those still trapped below."

"What do you need from me?" he asked, with no hesitation.

Leaning back, I let Michael take over. "We'll need schematics of the city and its defenses," he said. "We'll need all the information that can be gathered about the caverns, exits, routines, and guards. Any information that can be gathered about your government and its supporters that we can use against them and we'll need it within three days."

"It will be difficult, but not impossible to gather that, in fact, some I already have access to." Smiling at Tara's surprised look after stopping himself, he said, "I had no intention of our child growing up as a slave." Turning back to look at Michael, he continued. "The information about the caverns will be the most difficult to get. They keep everything about them well guarded. The rest, well, they are arrogant and do not view us as a threat."

Smiling grimly, Michael interrupted. "That's where you're wrong. They do view you as a threat and that's why they guard the truth about the caverns so zealously. Misty learned the truth of the caverns before she escaped and the truth is that there are hundreds of caverns filled with hundreds of thousands of your people in each one. They're down there right now wanting freedom. Didn't you know?"

A hardness entered his voice. "No, the first thing that is beaten into you when you're brought up here is to never mention the caverns or your life before the surface again." And now he knew why, if they had all been able to speak freely, they would have learned how many hadn't come from the same caverns. "The entrance to the caverns is located on the outskirts of the city, separate, but still within the wall. There is going to be a slave auction tomorrow—it will be the best time to enter that section. The area is under constant heavy guard."

"Are the guards soldiers like us?" Michael asked, indicating his uniform.

"No they are a segregated guard, they're only duty to guard the caverns and the slave auctions. They are unable to leave that area at any time and remain there until their deaths."

"Tehenis, can soldiers like us attend?"

"Yes, some even buy the female slaves, using them for a while before selling them to a brothel."

Looking at the window, I saw that it was starting to get light and that we had been here speaking longer than I realized. I butted in, "I think we need to wrap this up. Tehenis, are there others that you trust not to betray you and help to gather the information that we need?"

"Yes I managed to gathers several that feel as I do"

Smiling grimly "Good, get them to work and tell them to take great care. We'd rather leave without the information and try again than have them get caught and jeopardize the whole thing. Don't tell them about us—the less they know the safer we'll all be." Turning to Michael, I said, "I think we need to head back now and get some rest before we attend the auction."

"Agreed. Tehenis we'll meet you here tomorrow night." Getting up, at Michaels urging we murmured our farewells, replacing our helmets and exiting the house to wait outside for Tara, wanting to give the two of them a moment of privacy. The soft click of the door told us when she joined us and without looking back we walked away.

Chapter 18

I have now seen hell and its servants in their truest forms. When you are born and live within the caverns you know that your life is not your own. You know that each breath you take is numbered and that freedom is not yours. These poor wretches that stand before me have learned the truth, there is no freedom, only more pain to come. Though we are slaves within the caverns, we are protected by family and friends who are willing to take a beating or even die if it means that we are safe. Those that stand here in the hot sun have lost that. Poked and prodded, they whimper in fear as strange hands glide over them, checking their worth. The thoughts of those that touch them are plain to see. They move through line after line of the new crop, speaking about them as if they were no more than a piece of furniture.

We walked through the pavilions where they were displaying specialty stock, perfumed and pampered, the most unique that they gathered posed to look like dolls. The guards that surrounded them let the buyers know that these were look, don't touch. Men, woman, and children littered these booths, causing disgust to roll through me, but I ignored it, keeping a careful eye on my companions, who, though they have known injustice and have recently felt the pain that wrongful death brings, have not known the true depths of evil that the human soul is capable of. Looking at the children was the worst because I assumed that they were the orphan children and the lottery had stolen the last of their family. We had always assumed that they all became soldiers, but now I knew better.

As much as I'd have liked to help these wretches, that wasn't what I was here for. Moving through the crowd, I discreetly made my way toward what we had come to see. It was closer than I thought—it was only about a mile behind the house that stood behind the auctions were the slaves were brought when they were taken from the caverns. Guards were everywhere, but they appeared to be more concerned with the auctions than with manning their posts. Leaving the others, Michael and I broke off, knowing that we would be less likely to be caught. Cautiously, we made our way to the house, trying to blend in, which was easier than I thought. Though a few guards glanced at us, as soon as they saw the uniforms their gazes skirted away, going back to the main crowd. Luck seemed to be on our side when I spotted a pair of glass doors left slightly ajar, and ducking into them, we waited to make sure that we weren't spotted. After a few minutes we knew we were good.

The room was dark, but the light coming through the crack of the curtains made it light enough to see. We were in what appeared to be a sitting room. Quietly I walked to a door, cracking it open I saw that it led to a large foyer. Closing it, I motioned Michael to check the other door and I followed, hoping that it led to a less open floor plan. Jackpot. The door opened into an office and moving in, we split up, while Michael took the vid display and the desk, I went to a group of cabinets designed into the wall, curious as to what could possibly be in them. Empty, each one I opened was empty. Closing the last one, I stepped back, going over to Michael, who murmured my name. Stepping behind him, I looked over his shoulder, watching as he pulled up file after file—everything from the sales to the scheduling for the guards was there, but it wasn't really what we were looking for. Pulling a drive from his pocket, he attached it to a port in the vid display, copying the files to review later. As he worked, I kept being drawn back to the cabinets. Leaving Michael, I went back, opening each again and running my hands over them. Why would they just leave the cabinets empty, I thought, as my hands moved. Just as I was about to give up, it clicked, literally, my finger moved over a space like any other except this one gave way, sliding the cabinets to the side.

Whispering Michael's name, I stepped forward and lights came on as I moved in—they must have been motion activated. Another desk stood in the middle of the large room. Moving to it after a moment, Michael murmured "jackpot." Leaving him to his work, I went to the true cabinets along the sides of the room. Each had the contents and dates listed on the fronts. Pulling opening the ones I thought could be relevant, I began pulling out vid discs, putting them in the satchel I was carrying. Going deeper down the rows, I found cabinets that dated back hundreds of years. Stuffing my bag with everything I could find, I kept searching until I noticed a remote that looked like it went to a vid display. Pressing the button, the room came alive, screen after screen showed around the room of the interior and exterior of the house, showing that the house was much larger than it appeared. From what I could tell, it went deep into the ground, but that wasn't what truly interested me—zeroing in on one image in particular, I read and then reread the caption that showed across the screen: "Cavern slave intake." Going to Michael, something else caught my eye—we had people moving toward the office. Running, I grabbed Michael's arm, whispering urgently.

Rushing from the room, the lights shut off as soon as we left and the door closed automatically behind us, we had just made it to the adjoining room, our door closing when theirs opened.

Voices could be clearly heard from the other room, the words stopping us from making our escape. "Things are now moving faster and then we had anticipated. The escapees from the caverns have caused more problems than I dreamed possible," a male voice said.

"How does this concern me, Henil?" a female voice amusedly drawled.

"Well, President Bethel seems to not have finished killing those he believes responsible for this mistake. So if we don't want to find ourselves on the chopping block, we'd better find a way to be useful in fixing this mess," the man Henil growled.

"How can I be blamed?" she hissed.

"Oh, my dear, you above anyone should know how easily it is done, but I'm sure that it won't come to that if you work with me," he smoothly said.

"What do you require of me Henil?" she pushed out.

"I'll require some of your best trained slaves. You know, the ones that have been broken to the point that they will do anything you wish. The ones that report all their masters' secrets and business to you." Chuckling, he said, "My dear I know that your beauty fools those fools, but did you think that I didn't know your game? You live well beyond your means, my dear, so I would assume that you're little blackmail and secret selling enterprise has been extremely profitable for you."

"What do you need them for? What's your plan?" she asked, not bothering to deny his charges.

"The plan, my dear, is to release them into the wild and allow that fool rebel force to capture them. We need to find their base of operations and destroy it."

"Agreed that it must be destroyed, but how will we find them? I'm sure that they'll be checked before being allowed entrance and even those fools would watch closely," she told him.

"I'm aware of that, it's why they'll be implanted with trackers that are able to turn on and off once we are in range."

"Even if we destroyed the main rebel base, how does this help us? The people there now see us as a threat, we wouldn't be able to continue with the original plan to slowly take over their government and them," she mused.

"Yes, that is no longer an option for us. It is why in ten days we are preparing for a large strike. Our soldiers, disguised as ordinary citizens, are already being sent to the Stone City and outer provinces as guests of their government. The fools have even allowed our military access within their borders to search for our lying traitor." Chuckling darkly, he went on, "We won't even have to move more troops from the city, everything we need will already be there—they'll have no idea what is happening until it's finished. Their government and its official have been so easy to manipulate, their greed not letting them see what's in front of them."

A scraping noise had us pulling back from the door and racing to the outside quickly, checking to make sure that we wouldn't be seen leaving. Once out, we tried to move naturally, so we wouldn't draw attention, and rejoined the auction attendants. Making our way in farther, we went in search of the others. Passing groups bidding on slaves, we finally found them watching stonily the sale of a child. You could tell that they wanted to do something, but some harshly whispered words from Michael had them turning their backs and following us. No words were said as we took the transport back to our quarters. As the door clicked behind us and the lock was thrown firmly in place, he turned to Samuel and Tara with suspicion clear in his eyes before masking it.

"What time are we schedule to leave tomorrow?" he asked Samuel.

"Our transport is scheduled for six a.m. departure."

Nodding his head, he went to the food laid out on the table by the servants who had been here earlier.

"What did you find out?" his second-in-command asked, clearly confused by our silence.

"We managed to get into the main house and find some vid disc we won't know there value of until we're back at camp and are able to access them," he replied in a tone that said he was through discussing it. Keeping my face blank when they turned to look at me, I joined

Michael, picking at the fruits on the table. After everyone was seated, Michael began to speak again. "I don't want anyone leaving the unit. Tara, Misty, and I will go to Tehenis late in the night and collect anything he might have found, but other than that, I don't want to jeopardize our chance of getting out of this hellhole tomorrow. Now I want everyone to get as much rest as they can, we'll be driving in shifts, there will be no breaks if it can be helped. I have no intention of ending up like those people at the auction." Murmurs of agreement passed through the room as thoughts of what they had seen played through our heads. Death was better than the fate those poor beings were being forced to suffer.

Silently, the rest of our day passed into night, the day's events casting a morbid feeling through all present. Michael and his second-in-command were to the side, speaking in whispered words as he passed my satchel to him. They would take our bags and we would meet them at the transport after we finished with Tehenis. Turning my gaze to the direction of Tara and Samuel, I discreetly watched them out of the corner of my eye. Were they waiting for a chance to betray us or were they truly just looking to help free our people? We really knew nothing of them and I know that was the reason Michael wanted us to keep quiet about what we had seen and heard. As I stared on, the image of a golden-haired child at the auction flashed into my mind. Her little broken spirit that to me showed clearly in her desolate eyes and blank face sent a piercing pain into my ice-incased heart. It was that image that had me picking up a large tote when we left, hoping that I wasn't making a mistake that would cost any of us our lives.

The streets were just as alive as they were the other night though with a different type of people than those who roamed during the day. Tehenis met us at the door as if he had been watching, quickly shutting it behind us, gathering Tara into his arms. We had one hour before we were to depart, so he quickly showed us what he had been able to gather. Vid discs of the city's defenses and information on the population and infrastructure were given to us. It was more than we could have hoped for. Quietly we spoke as Michael passed him communications codes so that we could coordinate with him, knowing that us coming back to the city would be a risk if they found out what we had stolen. Time passed quickly and we needed to leave; going outside, we gave Tara and her husband a moment alone. When she joined us, you could tell that she was barely holding herself together. We hadn't walked a few steps when I told them that I had left my tote behind. Telling them to go ahead, I rushed back and got it, rejoining them fifteen minutes later. Ignoring their looks that spoke without words—asking what took me so long—I repositioned my bag across my back, holding the strap tightly in my grip and silently followed.

We joined the others just as they were about to enter the transport pick-up station. We waited as the man who ran the facility came forward and scanned Michael's tag. Looking down, he spoke into a device in his ear and a few moments later a vehicle was being brought around. No one spoke as we loaded our bags and ourselves in. Following Tara's directions, we maneuvered through the city reaching the final gate. I think we all held our breaths as the final scan was made when the large gates opened and we were able to cross the bridge and begin our journey back to the free world. No one released that breath until the trees surrounded us, as if welcoming us home.

Chapter 19

We would be home tonight. Passing more and more patrols that had seemed to grow exponential since we left, I worried that there may not be enough of us to fight. In less than an hour we would reach a different entrance to the bunker, one that would allow us to drive the vehicle right in. A diversion had been planned to draw any lingering troops in that area away. Stopping on the deserted stretch of road, we got out and went about disabling the vehicle's tracking system. Taking advantage of everyone leaving the vehicle, I went and checked my bag making sure that everything was still good. The sound of sudden silence had me pulling out my knife and moving into the shadows.

"You two watch them while I go and see what they're carrying. Maybe next time they'll think twice before not sharing some extra rations," a voice laughed harshly right before its owner stepped in.

Remaining completely still I blended into the wall as I watched the soldier approach, going toward the supplies we were carrying. Rifling through, he pulled a bottle of alcohol that must have been placed in there for the officers. Taking a large swig, he smiled as he looked around, poking at things until he came to our bags.

Unzipping my bag, he gave a little yelp as a pair of large frightened eyes stared back at him. It was the last sound that he'd ever make. Stepping forward, I wrapped my arm around him, covering his mouth with my hand before using my knife to cut his throat. Through it all I held the pair of eyes staring at me from the bag, willing her not to scream. Taking his weight with my body, I lowered him to the floor before stepping forward to re-zip the bag.

"Mason, keep the gun on them while I go see what's taking Peterson so long," a voice huffed as it came closer to the vehicle. Moving to the door, I pressed my body all the way back, waiting until he stepped in and was clear of the sight of the door before shoving my knife deep in his throat. Ripping it free, I watched as he gurgled for a moment before he was dead. Taking a look at the door, I could see that the last soldier's back was to me. Stepping from the vehicle, I approached him from behind, shoving my knife into the base of his head before he had a chance to turn. Stepping forward, Michael took the gun from his now limp grip before he fell to the ground.

Pulling my knife free, I heard the sound of an explosion in the distance. Racing to the vehicle, we threw the bodies out to the side of the road, unable to take the time to hide them. I could feel the others looking at me, but I ignored them, closing my eyes. A large bump had me reopening them, as I realized more time than I thought had passed—instead of the forest, thick concrete surrounded us, we were home. I hadn't bothered to really learn the names of my companions, so when one growled, "Why the hell did you do that? You should have just let them take the supplies. You could have ruined everything." I just looked at him, uncaring, before I stood. The sounds of footsteps of whoever was outside approaching could be heard in the loud chamber. Walking back to my large tote, I carefully took it down, placing it on the floor before unzipping it and letting out the little girl who had been hidden within. Though she was clinging to me, I stood with her in my arms and walked her over to an immobile Tara. Placing the little girl on her lap, I pried her fingers from my neck and placed them around Tara's. "This is your mother," I told her, before gathering my bags and walking by my stunned unit out the door.

Standing under the running water of the shower, I watched the red pool at my feet before going down the drain. The blood of my enemies washed clean from my body and soul. Stepping from the shower, I wrapped myself into a robe, going out of the small room. Michael sat in a chair watching me. Ignoring him, I went to the bed and sitting down, I rested my back to the wall and pulled my feet up, closing my eyes.

"Why?" he asked, breaking the silence.

Without opening my eyes, I said, "The father will be freer to help us now without concern for the child's fate if he is discovered."

"Why didn't you tell us that you had the child after we were away? You had to know we wouldn't have sent her back." He sighed.

Opening my eyes I tilted my head to look at him. "It was safer if no one knew. If we were stopped, someone might have appeared nervous. We were hiding enough secrets without adding that burden to the others."

"Why did you take her?" he asked, and I knew why he was asking.

With a humorless smile, I said, "I already told you. My plans haven't changed—I'm still planning to kill her mother." Seeing that he wouldn't let this go, I said, "If her father is killed, then she has no one. The government takes the children that have no one and they become soldiers or what you saw at the auction. At least here she will be given to another family to be raised. They didn't have to help and it's not just their lives at risk if they're caught, so I took the child to repay our debt to them." Standing, I went to the closet, pulling out some clothing. "Give me a moment to dress and I'll go with you to speak to the council. We don't have much time," I said, ending the subject. We had much more important issues to deal with than one child, so why did I risk all our lives to save hers?

Stepping into the large hall, it felt empty as it only held the council members and our military leaders. A private session was held to disclose what we had learned. "In five days' time, the city plans to attack and take us over," Michael said to the stunned audience. It had taken us longer to get back due to an issue with the vehicle. "They have been quietly setting up their soldiers in all the towns as regular visiting citizens, the invasion force is here and just waiting for the moment to strike."

"General Petro, where are we at with the training of our forces?" Samson said, taking Michael's warning to heart.

"We've had them training around the clock in shifts," he said, hardening his face. "I didn't know if it will be enough if they are going against hardened soldiers that have been trained for years."

Murmurs sounded around the room, stepping forward, I asked silencing the room. "What about your government's trained military troops?"

"That's the problem, they are the government's troops."

"Not necessarily, they are citizens first. Citizens whose family members will be in danger. If we could get in touch with their families, we may have a chance at getting them to stand with us." Seeing the blatant disbelief in their eyes, I tried another tactic. "The Loyalist city plans on completely overthrowing your government and making a slave out everyone left alive when the dust clears. Your government leaders are too stupid to realize that they are not going to remain in power after this coup. They will have most of your troops un-deployed, easily captured, or killed in their un-readiness. It would seem to me that the first strike that they would want to make is to get rid of your main defenses. Most of the troops are housed in two bases, one in the Stone City the other in Twin Rivers. I'll bet that is where the first strikes will take place. If we place our troops near enough, we should be able to save the majority of them and get those still alive to fight with us."

"It's not a bad idea," a dark-haired man said, looking at me thoughtfully. "We'd need to work out some details, but I think it would work. Especially if we could get some of their family members to join us. Most wouldn't hesitate to join us if they see a military threat against their civilian family members"—he raised his hand to stop a red-faced man from speaking—"I don't mean we take children to use as bait, but adults willing to fight for the cause," he finished, deflating the man's argument before it begun.

"We'll have to move fast if we have a chance of being in place before the fighting starts. And each town will have to be warned. We don't have enough weapons yet to arm everyone. I don't know if it just would be best if they didn't resist," Councilman Vincent said, looking troubled.

I knew what they were thinking. They were thinking of their own village and the senseless deaths. "Vincent, your people were unarmed and the soldiers didn't care. Do you honestly think if they don't fight that they will be spared until help can come? My government's soldiers have no honor or mercy in them. They were not raised by families, but by the state to be soldiers. It is better that those people fight with their bare hands if they have to. I say this to you now and heed my warning—there can be no mercy, if you show it or expect it, you will die. So think long and hard before taking surrendering soldiers; it's best just to go for the kill and be done with it."

"She's right, Vincent, its best that all of you heed her words. Those soldiers are little more than monsters. The things that we witnessed in that city will stay with me until my death, burned there by the depravity. I would gladly kill myself and any of our people that I could reach rather than let them take us as captives," Michael said, the horrors of his time in the city naked in his eyes for all to see.

"Then they fight," Petro said. "Is there anything else we should be aware of?"

"Yes, they are trying to plant spies among us. They're going to release them like Prey. They will be implanted with a homing beacon that can be turned on and off to avoid immediate detection," Michael said, causing a look to pass among them that I didn't like. "How many are already here?" he asked, interpreting their looks correctly. They must have flown them in to beat us back.

"Four, they're being rounded up now, sir," called our guard from the back of the hall who had sent out a warning as soon as the words left Michael's mouth.

"Have any unauthorized signals been monitored since their arrival?"

"Negative."

Looking at the soldier, an idea formed. "They're planning on taking us out first," I mused slowly, as things started to fall into place. "They have no idea where we are located, those spies, they were to lead them to us, but they assume that we are in the woods. Those extra patrols that we saw must be part of the group massing to take us out."

"That would make sense," Michael nodded.

"We could take them wherever we wanted and that's where the soldiers would go, to look for us."

Smiling, Michael approved. "Yes, they would. We could lead them anywhere or into anything."

Chuckling, Petro put in, "They'll be moved within the hour. Toward the ranges to the south, there's a lot of open space there and our demolition expert will have some practice."

After that they made plans on how to use the spies who were really no more than casualties of war. The talks over the next six hours ranged from how to infiltrate the Stone City to the outer towns. Everything that would take place over the next few days began in this room. There was no telling what the death toll would be when this was finished, but I knew that it would be more than they could imagine. I was exhausted when we finally finished for the night, the events of the last almost two weeks taking its toll.

Rising up, Michael caught my arm and held it to him as he spoke. "Dillon," Michael said to the dark-haired man from earlier, "has your division accessed the codes that I brought back yet?"

"They're working on it now. I'll let you know as soon as we're successful in gaining access to their internal video grid. They're poring over the vid discs you also brought back now to see if anything useful can be gained."

"Keep your men working on it. I have a feeling that if we can access their video system, we'll have a chance to hack their computer systems. I believe that it is all networked together in some way."

Dillon smiled tiredly, "After everything that was said tonight, we could use a break like that." Nodding his head to me, he said, "We'll talk more tomorrow—you'd better walk her to her room, she looks dead on her feet."

Without another word, Michael slowly turned me and walked me through the halls. It was a testament to how tired I was that I didn't protest when he led me like a child. As tired as I was, I knew that sleep would be long in the coming and short in the having—my past too close to the surface to allow for anything else. Opening the door, he led me into my room. Breaking away, I went to my bed, toeing off my shoes and curling into a ball. Opening my eyes when I felt him over me, I felt him lean down and remove my jacket, tossing it on the chair that held his. Scooting toward the wall when I saw him move to sit, I was surprised when he laid down and pulled me over, tucking my head under his chin and wrapping his arms around me. "Sleep," he whispered, and surprisingly, I did, in the comforting warmth of another person, pushing back the cold darkness that would have seized me had I been alone.

Chapter 20

We had moved the spies just in time. We were able
to reach the area that had been approved and our trap was
successful. A part of the large contingent of the soldiers
that had been searching in this area were now dead, the
explosives having killed over two hundred of them.
Heavily armed, they were sitting ducks as they searched for
an entrance that did not exist. The ones that had survived
the explosion hadn't returned to this area. Everyone here
had basked in the announcements of those deaths, their
need for vengeance in the name of those that they had lost
was a thirst that the water from the deepest well could not
quench.

Moving through the corridor, I went to have a
private meeting with Vincent before I left. The day after
tomorrow the battle would begin and our troops had been
moving in small groups in preparation. Some were sent to
warn the outlying villages and towns while others
infiltrated the Stone City or scouted the forests to see where
the soldiers hid and where to hide our troops in preparation
to take the military bases. These people had not truly seen
war since the great cleansing, so I knew that the excitement

that they now felt would turn quickly to ash as their loved ones never returned to them again.

Not bothering to knock, I entered his office, taking a seat in front of his desk. "I hear that you are going to the Stone City," he stated, coming right to the point.

"Yes, I felt that I would be more useful there," I replied, even though he didn't expect an answer.

Pulling off his glasses, he rubbed between his eyes, "We have better uses for you than dying. We expect heavy casualties in the assault to take the Stone City. It would be a loss to the cause if one of them was you."

"There are more manageable bodies from the cavern here and in the city—pick one of them to be the figure head for the revolution."

"More manageable, yes," he snorted, before looking at me, his voice grave, "but more respected, no. Did you know that your name is whispered in every town, village, and city?" I shook my head, while he continued. "It has come to have the same meaning as freedom. One day, hopefully soon, it will be whispered among the people of your caverns, they'll know that you stood up when no one else would. The men and woman that rush to join us come to fight for you. You represent what was lost all those years ago. A willingness to fight and die not because you have something to gain, but because it is the right thing to do."

"I'm not a hero and I'm sure as hell not going to be a martyr if I can help it. I don't want to be the reason they fight," I said angrily.

Smiling sadly, he said, "You, child, are a beacon in the darkest night, you stand there guiding us all from the darkness. A darkness that descended over this land thousands of years ago when in an act of greed and vengeance the evil of man destroyed it rather than admitting that they were wrong. The dust eventually settled, life returned, and the sun rained its rays down upon the land once more, but the darkness of that deed has never left. We made peace with evil rather than fight for what we knew to be right. We turned an eye from the suffering of our own, afraid that if we acted, we would join them. We live in shame not because we did something, but because we did nothing. Then you, a girl that had everything to gain by her silence, stood up and spoke out loudly and said what in our shame we didn't. I know that you don't see it, but what you have begun has spread far and wide burning a blaze of righteousness across these lands and our people's hearts. They can no longer hide in ignorance, but must step out and join you in the light of truthfulness that no darkness can hide." Pointing at me, he said, "You are the brightest star that blazes in the sky, guiding them on their journey in the darkest, most moonless night. You are still there, seen by all, revered because you can do what no other has, unite our people once more and guide them to freedom."

Pain and fear moved though me at his words. "I didn't ask for this. I don't want it, I'm not a leader," I denied, standing up and going to the door. Opening it, I froze at his next words.

"Greatness is not asked for, it is given to those who can carry the burden," he said, leaning back into his chair. "You will go to the Stone City and fight. I know you well enough to know that you would never have stayed out of it. I just ask that you remember one thing, death is easy; it's life that is hard."

"That, Victor, is lesson that I never have to be reminded of," I replied, closing the door and swiftly making my way through the hall.

Ignoring the smiles thrown at me, I tried not to run as I went toward a small side exit. I needed to be outside this place that was crushing me. I didn't want the burden of another life. Three had been in my keeping and I had not been able to save even one. Now he tells me thousands upon thousands are my responsibility. He was insane if he thought that I would accept this. Let another bear the pains of their deaths, I had no more room inside me. Finally reaching the door, I ordered the guard to open it, impatient when he checked to make sure it was safe. As soon as there was enough room, I pushed myself through, unable to wait. Racing forward, I blindly went into the woods.

The whips of the branches smacked me as I rushed forward, raising my hands to protect my face. I welcomed the pain that each hit brought to my arms. Running until I felt as if my heart would burst, I collapsed into a useless pile. Why couldn't they leave me alone? I didn't ask for any of this. I wasn't even supposed to be alive. I should have died in the caverns instead of the girls. I should have been the one taken in the village instead of Tristian. I should have died a hundred times in the place of those I'd loved. I should have died for the lives I've taken and yet here I was. A broken shell whose hate and pain was too deep to show. This was what they wanted to stand there as inspiration. Wrapped in my own pain that Victor's words had set free, I didn't hear Michael's approach. When he gathered me him his arms, I didn't open my eyes, uncaring who it was, just wishing that it was finally over. That he had finally come to end it and set me free. Opening my eyes, I looked and whispered a tormented "please." Please set me free, I silently begged with my eyes.

Instead of heeding my unspoken words, his eyes turned hard and he stopped rocking me. "Please?" he asked, deceptively soft. Closing my eyes, wanting to block him and the world out, I wasn't given that option. A firm hand gripped my face, squeezing until I relented and looked at him. "Please what? Let you run into the woods to be captured or please let you die?" he asked, again in a deceptively soft voice.

"Yes, both, either, I don't care," I dully answered, already moving away mentally since he would not let me go physically.

As if he sensed my retreat, he jerked my face sharply, causing me to focus on the hard lips descending to mine. Roughly, they consumed my mouth, forcing me to react, to feel. Unable to retreat, I pushed forward giving to him as hard as he gave to me. Raising my arm, I dug my fingers into his hair gripping hard. I wanted him to hurt as I hurt. I wanted him to hurt me as I hurt him just so I could feel. Pushing myself up, I toppled us, rolling around in the grass, leaves, and dirt until I lay flat on my back with him tightly pressed above me. With angry hands, I pushed his jacket from his body so he could feel my nails as I dug them into him. Ripping and pulling at one another, I reveled in it, loving the pain. Completely in the moment, I felt the exact second when it changed. Gentling the kiss, he forced me to comply. Pulling my hands between us, he held them still with one hand and my face with the other. Moving from my lips he placed feather kisses on my face, moving to my neck.

What I had been trying to escape came back, firmly dancing before my eyes, but I was in control now, my calm façade back in place. "Michael, let me up, we have to go." Resting his forehead into my neck, we sat like that until our breath evened out and heartbeats were steady once more. In a fluid motion, he rose up, pulling me with him. Silently we walked side by side. We walked back not touching. Reaching the door, the guard opened it and I entered, leaving him to go where he would while I gathered my bag and headed down to the transportation room. We would be going in as soldiers. There were enough currently roaming in the Stone City and Twin Rivers that we would just blend in.

Chapter 21

The roads were almost deserted; something wasn't right. It was late into the night when we made it to Twin Rivers and hadn't passed one checkpoint. The streets were empty at this hour and the silence was eerie. Parking our vehicle, we made our way on foot the last few blocks to the safe house. The place was pitch black when we entered and turning on the light, we found Johnathon slumped face-down in a pool of blood on the floor. Rushing to him, I carefully rolled him over while the others moved to check the area to make sure that we were safe to stay here. The moan that he gave was music to my ears. Getting up, I rushed to the sink and got a bowl of water. Sitting down, I put his head into my lap and wiped the blood from his face. Looking up, I saw Michael and another standing there motioning for me to move. Scrambling out of the way, I hovered as they lifted him up and put him on a bed. Once they stepped back, I moved forward and removed his shirt. His body was worked over so badly I didn't know how he made it here, never mind how he was still alive.

For an hour Michael and I worked together fixing what we could. Once his ribs were wrapped and the final stitch put in, Michael brought an injection to Johnathon's neck, unable to wait for answers any longer. Pain clouded his eyes as he opened them. He gazed around the room unseeing, until he landed on Michael. Sharp focus entered his eyes as his hand snaked out, encircling Michael's wrist and tugging him forward. "They know," he hoarsely pushed out. Picking up a glass for water, I slowly fed it to him, stopping when he made to turn his head away. Clearing his throat, he tried again, "They know that we know about the attack." Pulling his weak body up, he continued. "They've pushed it up, it will begin at dawn. The attack will begin at dawn," he got out, before releasing his grip on Michael and collapsing back, wheezing in pain.

Watching as they all raced around, I felt the horrors of those words resonate through me—they knew. The attack would happen at dawn and we weren't prepared. They were trying to raise the main base to warn them, but couldn't get through. All signals were being jammed. Rushing over to Michael, I said, "We have to try to get someone out of here to warn the others. That's why it was so easy to get in—they want us in. They want us here trapped."

Calling over the two men by the door, he said, "Hanson, Ellis, we need you to try and get out of the town, deep into the forest, where you can broadcast a signal."

Their "yes, sirs" were still in the air as they picked up the equipment that they would need and silently slipped into the night. There was almost no chance that they would make it, we all knew it, but we still needed to try. There was only five hours left until dawn and when that happened all hell would break lose. How did they know? How did they know? Going back to Johnathon, I could see he was fighting to remain conscious. Kneeling down, I asked, "How did they know?" hoping that he was lucid enough to answer. When all I got was silence, I started to rise. "The spies," he whispered. Quickly kneeling back down, I asked, "What spies?"

"You moved the spies," he said, before losing himself to unconsciousness, causing it to click in my mind. The spies the city sent to infiltrate the bunker. How would that matter unless… "Michael," I strangled out, "they know."

"What are you talking about?" he asked, not bothering to look up from the map he was poring over with the others.

"They know we were there."

"What are you talking about? I don't have time for this."

Standing up, I walked over and stood across the table from him. Slamming my hands down, I said, "They know that we were in the city. Somehow they know. They knew that we knew about the Prey, now either someone within has betrayed us, or they knew we were at the Loyalist city," I yelled, my chest heaving, my eyes wild. Taking a deep breath, I said, "so either you didn't erase us off the video like you thought or we have a traitor within our command unit, because everyone we sent out was vetted and we still didn't tell them what was going on. They only thought that they were going to spy, not getting their true orders until tomorrow."

"That means that the bunker could be in danger."

"Yes. We have to help them."

"We can't."

Looking around at the others, their heads bowed, I couldn't believe what he said. "What do you mean we can't? Most of the troops have been sent out, making their way to their orders, all that's left down there is just a small group of troops, women, children, and the old—they'll be slaughtered."

Raising his face up to look into mine with stark emotion, he harshly whispered, "Do you think we don't realize that? Do you think that we don't know that our families are down there, all but defenseless?" Hardening his voice, he straightened, "We can't help them. We can't help anyone unless we can figure out a way to organize the troops we have in the town and city and take it before daybreak. So you telling us about the deaths of our families isn't helping. If you want to help, shut up and figure out a way that doesn't include the complete slaughter of our people. If you can't do that, go over there and wallow in what can't be changed, but either way, we have work to do," he spat out, dismissing me and turning back to the map.

Stepping back from the table, I walked past them and straight out the door into the brisk night air. Going deep into the shadows, I let the silence surround me as the truth of his words sunk in. I had let my emotions rule me and made an impossible situation worst. This was why I never opened myself to people—I didn't want to care. Caring meant that you could get hurt because the truth was that above or below there was nothing that you could to do to help. That's why I've always stayed to myself, pushing everyone that ever meant anything to me away, so that I could protect myself from the pain of knowing that no matter what I did, I couldn't save them. My self-pity wouldn't help me or anyone else for once. I needed my emotions and the logic they brought. That's what I needed––I needed to remember that it wasn't one group that mattered, but the whole and what the whole needed was each other.

Getting up, I went back in, ignoring the side looks I received and going straight to Johnathon. "Wake up," I said, shaking him hard. I slapped him across the face. "Wake up!" I yelled into his ear until he blearily opened his eyes. "Where did this happen?" I demanded.

"Lets me rest," he mumbled.

I didn't have time for this, shaking him hard, I asked, "Where were you attacked?"

This time, his eyes were more focused. "The town barracks."

"Who attacked you?"

"City soldiers."

"Did any of your troops survive?"

"Yes, locked below. They never had a chance," he answered, his words coming quicker as his mind worked through his pain.

"We can't get a signal out. Did you notice any equipment when you were escaping?"

"No, I was too busy running."

"Were you still receiving transmissions before you were attacked?"

"Yes," he said, more slowly this time. I was losing him.

"Johnathon, I need you to stay with me just a moment longer, OK?" I said. When he moved his head in as much of a nod as he could, I went on. "Do you know if they took the city guard or if they stopped with you?"

"Just us, I heard them say that they were taking the city tomorrow," he slurred, before drifting back into sleep.

Squeezing his shoulder, I stood up and left him to his rest, turning to the others who were glaring at me. Justin, the one next to Michael, sneered at me, saying, "It's bad enough that you want to kick us when we're down, but to beat on an already beaten man, it's no wonder your government treats you like animals, that's what you are."

Taking a deep breath, I took the hate he has throwing at me in, allowing it to feed my own. "What I was doing was finding out if the soldiers' base of operation was in the town. Which means that the transmission blocker is in that building with them, along with armed troops that will gladly join us. Not nearly as important as staring at a map and wondering where is the best spot to make your last stand, I know, but an animal like myself isn't going to roll over and die, we're going to bite the hand before it has a chance to beat us," I told him coldly, going and gathering what I would need. Throwing the bag over my shoulder, I went for the door.

"Where do you think you're going?" Michael said, gripping my arm. "We need to come up with a plan— rushing out there will only get you killed."

The coldness in my voice turned to frost. "I have a plan. I'm going to turn myself in."

The harsh shake he gave me told me before he opened his mouth that he wasn't pleased. "Turn yourself in, then what, get killed while taking a few of them out and losing the element of surprise for the rest of us?"

"No, Michael, it will get me in there close enough to use this jammer," I said, swiping it from the packs, and waving it in his face, "which will give you enough time to get a message out." I yanked my arm from his grip. The tick in his jaw told me that he wanted to argue, but my plan was sound. Going with the advantage his silence was giving me, I said, "I'll scout the area. Send your men out to gather as many as they can to help after your guy there"—I pointed to the guy still twisting knobs—"gets the message out that your group will attack. They'll be distracted by me so it will give you the element of surprise. Take the guards outside down quietly and the ones on the inside won't know what hit them."

"Do you understand what they'll do to you?" he quietly asked.

"Guess Victor was right," I said, with a small grim smile. Opening the door, I said, "In one hour I go in. Have your men in place by then." Quietly closing the door behind me, I headed into a connecting alley. I had a pretty good sense of direction and from the map what I was looking for should be in this direction. I needed a vantage point and a few alleys over I found a ladder that took me up a building tall enough to get a decent view. Keeping my body low, I looked out and waited, I didn't have long. Watches had been placed on four roofs surrounding the barracks, which was typical. They'd have to be removed if the others had a chance—the only reason I saw them was because I knew what I was looking for from years of experience. To Michael and his men, their eyes would just glaze over them as if they were fixtures of the buildings.

Carefully going back down, I allowed what the cavern had made me to come forth. I knew that the others thought that that the first lives I had taken had been in the service of the rebellion, but they couldn't have been more wrong. Life in the cavern was not for the squeamish and those who were not ready and willing to do what they must weren't the ones who survived. A young pretty girl left on her own to wander was something the more dark-hearted below couldn't pass up. Fissures and crevices are filled with the unlikely who thought to take what I wasn't willing to give or had what I need for my family to survive. I wasn't a killer without reason, but I was a survivor for a reason. I could turn off my emotions and become what I needed to be when I needed it. And at this moment, it was more a blessing than the curse, what was left of my heart felt it was.

With silence I moved, becoming a part of the shadows that I was. Scaling the building walls was no different than doing so on the cavern walls. My hands and feet found unerringly each hold to help my climb. There was no hurry in my movements even though time was running out. To each building I made my way, leaving unseeing eyes behind at each spot I visited. Finally finished, I took as many as I dared on my way in on the ground, knowing that they wouldn't be missed until it was too late. At my last kill, I stopped, leaving my bag and weapons that I couldn't hide. The jammer was a small piece that shouldn't be too hard to hide, but it had to be in a spot I could still reach if my hands were bound. I wouldn't be able to turn it on until I was inside and all eyes were on me; if I did it any sooner, they would just reconfigure and all of this would be for not. Tucking the piece into my hair that was held up tightly, I'd learned long ago that it wasn't a place that others thought to search and the heavy mass had been an advantage to me on more than one occasion.

Chapter 22

It was time. Moving to the center of the street, I held my hands up and out to the side, walking to the very people I had spent my life trying to escape. They saw me, but before they could start using the device to see if there were others and learn what I had done, I called out. "I heard that you were looking for me. My name is Misty and I am the other escapee from the caverns." Bingo, dropping their hands, they gripped their guns tightly, yelling orders on where to place my hands and how to move. There was excitement in their voices that they couldn't hide. Yeah, I'm sure that there was a large reward for my capture, so they weren't going to spread the word; they were just going to bring me in. The fools never thought to wonder how I made it to them. The last soldiers before the barracks without being seen, their greed doing just what I knew it would. These where supposed to be the watchers. The commander of the force here would not want to alert the town to the true size of their presence, so most were likely kept inside.

With these two in there with me, nothing would stand in the others' way. Even if the other soldiers I was sure were hiding in the woods waiting to move on this town and the city that stood behind it heard and tried to help, they'd never make it. Not in time to help these soldiers or stop the city barracks from hearing the shots and taking the element of surprise away. The shove at my back brought me back to the now as the barrack doors were opened and I was pushed through, falling to my knees. The building was just as large as it appeared on the outside. The whole floor was one big open space and I was now in the front of it, as close to two hundred soldiers turned to look at me—about a hundred more than I expected to have been snuck into the town without notice. I wasn't getting out of here alive and if the others tried to come in and get me out, the only resistance in this town would die with me. I let none of this show on my face as I was roughly gripped, pulled up, and tugged between the two eager soldiers. Speculative eyes watched me as I was brought through them, my eyes taking in everything without appearing to. I was right; the equipment that was blocking the signals was here. Careful to not be seen looking, I moved my eyes, trying to find the only thing that might get me out of here, but I shouldn't have bothered. When I was thrown down in front of a man that I assumed was the commander, the door was plainly there to see, not far behind him.

Keeping my eyes straight ahead, I didn't even flinch when I heard the loud smacking sound next to me. "We don't have time for entertainment and I have no patience for soldiers abandoning their posts," the commander said in a bored voice, totally making a mockery of the violence that he just did. This was a dangerous man.

"Sir, it's not like that. This girl is the cavern escapee that we've been looking for," the soldier to my right said—the one who hadn't just been smacked.

"We thought that you would want her immediately, sir," the one to my left put in, not about to be forgotten in my capture.

A soft hand gripped my chin and lifted my face. Keeping my gaze dead, I looked into a gaze deader than mine. His thumb caressed me and a smile moved across his lips. "You, my dear, have been a naughty girl. What do you have to say for yourself?"

I knew that this would hurt, but I needed to move things along. I let my mask drop and life move into my eyes, locking them to his. Letting a smile curve my lips, I moved my face into his caress turning it until my lips grazed his thumb. Widening my parted, smiling lips I struck hard, biting down till I felt blood releasing. I was ready for the hand that came at my face, letting it throw me to the ground. Kicks rained onto me, and using the distraction I activated the device, than started to laugh. The kicks stopped as I knew they would, these bastards too curious for their own good. Rolling over, I pulled myself back to my knees, keeping my smile through the blood and pain. Tilting my head back I gazed at the commander, the sick bastard's expression never changed as he gazed at me with that dead look. "You've been too long from the caverns, my dear, and have forgotten your place," he said.

Raising a finger, I wiped at the dripping blood coming from my lip before bringing it to my mouth and letting my tongue dip out to taste it. "Now, commander, why ever would you think that?"

What must pass for a true smile of anticipation curved his lips. "I thought that we had beat the last of resistance from you cattle long ago. I have to admit that I like the fact that I'll have to break you to get what I want."

Needing to keep the focus on me, I said, "You would think, commander, that one little slave escaping from the caverns wouldn't make a difference in the grand scheme of things."

Giving me a thoughtful look, he said, "Yes, I have to admit that the fact that you and the male have caused such a disturbance has been quite unexpected. Somehow the two of you have managed to destroy centuries of planning in a very short time." Running his hand across my cheek like he was petting me, he added, "I am curious to know how you found that fissure to escape from and where it came out at."

"Just lucky, I guess. Your soldiers chased us right into it."

A sharp smack hit my check before he started caressing it again. "My dear, let us make a little deal, you and I. You don't lie to me and I shan't cut off pieces of your lovely body."

"Now, commander, let's not lie to one another."

Inclining his head, he said, "So true, my dear, my apologies."

"Well, commander, what is the plan for this little get together?"

Chuckling, he said, "For you, my dear, why you are to be sent back to the city for a short, painful visit. For these people, we're going to slaughter them and whatever's left of the population when we're finished will be kept to do the farming and manufacturing that we have been forced to trade for. Many of our people will be glad for the change of scenery. Our population is overcrowding and we need to expand our territory—this seemed the logical solution. Why should we build when everything is here for the taking?"

Seeming to consider his words, I said, "These people have been free, do you really think it will be so easy?"

"These people are your people, my dear, and as you know, your people adjusted to slavery quite easily. I expect that these ones shall be no different. Like the ones in the caverns, I'm sure that a few shall be trouble makers, but the traitors among them shall make them easy to identify." Releasing my chin, he sat down in the chair behind him, never taking his eyes from me.

"Speaking of traitors, how did you find where Tristian and I were hiding?"

A dry laugh left his throat. "Ah, my dear, haven't you figured it out yet? I would have thought that you'd know by now. But, then again, that old man is quite good—he has been playing both sides for so long, I'm sure that he even believes his lies by now." He smirked and went on, "though the bastard thinks he could betray us now that he managed to gather this little rebel force, but what he failed to realize was that he wasn't the only spy that we had among you. It's how we found out that you knew of our little attack to come and moved it up."

A shadow moved past the window to my right, telling me that time was up. Rising to my feet, I stood in front of the commander, only the wave of his hand stopping the soldiers from knocking me back down. "Well, commander, it has been wonderful speaking with you and I truly hope that you survive so that we can continue our conversation," I said, giving him my darkest smile. There was no way that I was going to die now or not be victorious, no matter how many of them there were. I had unfinished business. Reaching up, I pulled the jammer from my hair and threw it at his feet. The smile slowly dropped from his face as he looked at it. Moving to my hair once more I pulled out what looked like a stick from the top that was holding my hair up. Turning just the right spot with my thumb twice, I smiled at the whizzing sound that it made. "But, then again, either way you've already given me what

I needed," I said, before throwing the grenade behind me into the mass of soldiers and throwing myself to the ground.

Wide-eyed, he had no chance to say anything before the explosion rocked the room, sending his men flying in every direction. My ears were ringing as the sounds of gunfire began to echo. Pushing the dead soldier that landed on me off, I tried to get my bearings. The rebels had stormed the building, killing any that they could. Pulling myself to my feet, I kept low as I made my way to the door that represented our only hope of winning. So focused was I on my goal that I didn't see the commander until it was too late. Throwing himself into me, we both fell hard to the ground. Taking the brunt of the impact, my breath rushed from my body, leaving me stunned long enough for his fist to tangle in my hair and slam my face into the floor. Pain shot through me, disorientated, I clawed at the hand behind me, causing a curse to leave his lips. When he slammed me down again, I saw stars. Flipping me over, he straddled me and encircled my throat with his hands. Fear raced through me as I fought for breath, his smiling face gloating down at me as a black spot swam in front of my eyes. Smacking, hitting, clawing at him only caused him to tighten his grip. A glint caught my eye from the corner and reaching out, I fought to grasp it. My bloody hand grazed it again and again, unable to catch it—I was going to die.

A tear fell from my eye as I realized that I had lost, after everything that I had done to survive, this was going to be it. As if reveling at my display of defeat, he leaned down and licked my falling tear, brought his lips to my ear, and said, "I would have loved to spend more time with you, my dear. The little that I was able to spend with your friend gave me quite a rush. We're only given you cave dwellers after you've been properly trained, so I never realized the spirt that they had to break to get you there." He chuckled, causing rage to infuse me, the bastard. Using the last bit of my strength, I bucked my hips up hard, moving him just enough so that I was able to reach the bottle. Grasping it, I brought it across the side of his head as hard as I could. He fell from me and I gasped at the sudden release of his hands, trying to pull in air to my denied lungs. Flipping myself over, I fought to get to my knees. This bastard had tortured Tristian—he was probably the leader of the unit that captured him and killed those people. Crawling through the blood to a fallen soldier, I threw myself over him, desperately clawing for what I needed. A hand slammed into my head, gripping my hair tightly and swinging me around. On my knees I was forced to look up, his face was a mess. The piece of the glass from the bottle was still there, deep in his eye and I smiled at the sight. Enraged by my amusement, he screamed, "Bitch," wildly lunging for my neck. Meeting his lung I swung the arm behind my back around, taking the knife that I pulled from the corpse and imbedding it to the hilt in his chest.

The momentum of my hit had thrown him back with me sprawled atop. Blood gurgled from his mouth as his hate-filled eye met mine. Pulling myself up, I tugged the knife free, causing his body to spasm and spit blood. Wiping the blade across his chest, I gripped the top of his uniform and pulled him up until we were nose to nose. "This is for Tristian," I whispered, right before taking my knife and running it across his throat. Dropping his body, I sat there on my knees slowly looking around. I was behind the enemy line. Michael's troops were fighting, but there were too many for them to win. Gripping the post next to me, I pulled myself up and stumbled toward the door. Reaching it was the hardest thing I had ever done, and with blood-slick hands I fumbled with the bolt until I was finally able to throw it clear. Opening the door, I think I shocked the troops when they saw the blood-soaked thing releasing them. "If you want to live than you have to fight," I said. Stunned, they still looked at me. "Now!" I roared, spurring them to action. Moving from their path, I slid down the wall and watched as wave after wave of them poured out. With bare hands they attacked the unaware city soldiers from behind. Now fighting two fronts caged in the middle, they hadn't stood a chance. The battle, harsh and unforgiving, was over in minutes.

Watching the troops gather the few still living surrendering soldiers and bring them toward the room that I had just released them from at Michael's orders forced me to my feet. Standing firm, I made my way over, blocking their path. Taking the gun from one of the troop's hands, I raised it and shot the soldiers in the head. After another eleven out of the twelve fell to the ground, I ignored Michael's shouts to stop. Placing the gun back into the troop's hand, I looked into Michael's face that was now right in front of me. "Question that one, now that he knows what will happen, he'll be more forthcoming with his answers." Turning without another word, I made my way to a door off to the side of the room.

Chapter 23

Stepping over the bodies, I could hear Michael yelling orders, trying to prepare the troops for the soldiers that would soon be joining us. Reaching the door, I went directly to the sinks, careful to avoid looking at the mirrors. Turning the water on, I brought my hands under, smiling grimly as I thought of how easily blood washes off. No matter how much is spilled, water will take it away like it had never been there. In slow, studied movements, I cleaned my hands and arms before leaning down to clean my face, careful of the gash I could feel on my forehead. Running my hands over my neck, the water ran down my shirt, causing small bloody drops to rain from me. Ripping a piece of my shirt at the bottom, I brought it under the water, rinsing it until the water that rained from it was clear. Bringing it up, I held it to the gash, wanting to stop the blood from running into my eyes when I stood up. Holding it as firmly as I could, I straightened, finally allowing myself to look into the mirror. Nothing stared back at me, not pain, not regret, nothing. Moving my eyes, I caught Michael's who stood behind me. "Where are we at? Were you able to get the messages out to warn everyone?"

"Yes, everything went as planned," he said in a clipped tone.

Not having the patience to deal with this, I turned to face him. "I did what had to be done. These people understand one thing and that is strength. Mercy is the same as being weak, so I did what you wouldn't do. We're out of time," I said, finished with the issue. "What's the new plan? What team am I with and where am I going?"

"You're not going anywhere, you're a mess. Go to the medic, he's waiting to take a look at you," he told me, and with barely suppressed anger he turned and walked away.

Moving forward, I followed him out, going to the medic and letting him do what he could for the gash to stop the bleeding. Refusing the painkiller, I watched as the groups left were being given their orders. Most of the troops had already been sent out to take positions to defend the town against the soldiers that were even now moving in. These last groups will be headed into the city to help hold it against the soldiers that had already infiltrated. Murmuring my thanks, I walked to the door, going out into the night. Townspeople were running through the streets as troops directed them to shelters. The ones they consider old enough to fight were armed and sent in a direction to join a unit. Their terror at what was to come could almost be tasted in the air. Following the path I had taken to get here, I went and got my bag. Moving out of the alley, back onto the main road, I saw Michael charging up.

Ignoring him, I walked ahead, straight past him, stepping out of the reach of the hand that tried to grab me. "You're not going out, you'll be a risk to your unit with your injuries," he said firmly. Whatever else he was going to say was stopped by the sound of bombs exploding at the edge of town. It had begun.

Pushing myself from the wall and him off of me, I turned. "I'm either going to a unit or I'm going out by myself, it's your choice," I said, watching his unit race toward us from the barracks.

Instead of answering me, he said, "Malice, Reshian, take point. Let's move." Motioning to one of the troops, he nodded and threw me the extra gun on his shoulder. Moving out, we raced in the direction of the Stone City. With the defenses back up, the air support that the soldiers had been planning on using were as good as a death sentence. It would be a ground battle and it raged. Though we were behind the line, bombs and bullets flew through the air. Hundreds of the Loyalist soldiers surrounded the town. The numbers were greater than was expected on all fronts. The fact that they were able to get so many so easily within the borders just testified to how high up the traitors within the rebellion were. The only hope the other villages and towns had was that the majority of the soldiers had been concentrated here, to capture the government's seat of power and the largest town.

I slammed to the ground as the building in front of us exploded, sending flying stone in all directions. I looked around to see if others had survived. One by one they rose from the debris to the deafening silence. It didn't last long, the western line had fallen and troops rushed toward us, falling back as the soldiers pursued. Raising our weapons, we fired, giving cover to the retreating troops. For every one we killed, two took their place—there were too many. Falling back to the line the troops had formed, we fought, hiding behind buildings and fallen stone for cover. The dead fell around us like rain; soon there wouldn't be enough of us left to make a difference. Michael was yelling, giving the orders to retreat when they came. Pouring from shelters and buildings, the townspeople that had been sent to hide raced forward. Barely a weapon among them, they swarmed the soldiers, taking them down by sheer numbers. With knives and rocks, they attacked, ripping the guns from the fallen. The surviving troops raced forward to help, pushing back the outnumbered soldiers.

Seeing Michael's signal, what was left of our unit followed him, racing through the war-torn streets. Ducking and dodging, we avoided the fighting when we could, embracing it when we couldn't. Finally we reached the bridge to the Stone City, where the fighting was intense. Grabbing Michael's arm, I signaled for the unit to stop; we'd never make it across. Moving away, I pulled my bag from the ground and dug out what I needed while the others covered me. Searching the ravine, I found what I was looking for, and aiming, I fired. The hook stuck true and pulling it tight, I raced to the firmest structure still standing and shot the other end in. Sure that it would hold, I yelled, "This is the only way!" Taking my rifle, I put it over the wire, gripping the ends than ran for it. Shots blazed around me, hitting my arm, but I held firm as I launched myself from the edge of the ravine into nothingness. Already weak from blood loss, the new hole that I sported made it worse. Once my feet began to dangle over ground instead of air, I held on as long as I dared before dropping. Pain jarred my body at the impact, but I pushed through it, gripping my gun and going to a rock cluster, firing to give the others cover.

One by one they joined me, taking my spot when Michael pulled me back to wrap my arm. Once he was finished doing what he could, he moved forward, taking control. We were pinned down, so pulling out my last trick from my bag, I threw it, smiling grimly at the screams that followed the explosion. Racing forward, using the distraction, we broke free and were able to make it into the outer part of the city. Death was everywhere. Those who could not fight and hadn't found safety in time laid in the streets their unseeing eyes bringing back memories of the field. Little ones huddled together in terror behind mothers who had tried to protect them. For a moment I was back in the caverns, frozen in terror as death surrounded me, before I was slammed to the ground as the world around me exploded. Looking over my shoulder, I was surprised at who I saw. "I thought that you didn't like me." I said.

Justin gave me a cocky grin, "You've kind of grown on me," he said, pulling me to my feet. "Come on!"

Nodding my head, I raced forward, joining Michael, who took precious seconds to look back to make sure I was OK. Mouthing "all good," he looked like he wanted to beat me. With a shake of his head, he refocused on the battle. The capitol building could be seen from where we were. The city's troops were doing well having heard us take the town's barracks, they were prepared when the soldiers attacked. They were fighting like there was no tomorrow and there really wasn't if they didn't win. Looking around, I spotted our route. "Follow me," I yelled, and racing forward I used the building for cover, moving until we came to an alley that we could barely fit in. Using the two buildings, I braced my back to one and feet to another, using the leverage to work my way up. After watching me for a moment, the others followed. "I'm beginning to think that you cavern dwellers are part monkey," Justin joked, as he struggled to keep up.

Before I could answer, the sound of someone approaching silenced us. Rooted to our spots, a unit of soldiers came down our alley, followed by perusing troops. Stuck above, a battle raged below—if they looked up, we were sitting ducks. We were more than halfway up; we had to take the chance. Signaling with my hands, I pointed up, ignoring the shaking head. Moving as quickly as I dared to, so not to dislodge any rocks, the others saw no choice but to follow, silently cursing me with their eyes. Pulling myself over the lip, I helped the others as they made it. The others secured the roof as I waited for Justin, gripping him when he was in reach and pulling him up and over the lip. Going down to the section that the soldiers were held up at, I sat down and began kicking until I dislodged the loose lip, sending it raining down upon them. Satisfied at their screams, I joined the others who were anything but happy with me. "Now what?" Michael growled, pointing around.

Securing the rifle across my back, I moved away from the edge of the roof. Once I gave myself enough room, I went for it. Racing forward, I propelled myself off the lip, flying through the air and landing on the next roof. One by one, the others joined me. "You know, I think that I'm back to hating you now," Justin growled as he pulled himself up.

"Believe it or not, that's not uncommon," I said, laughing at his mumbled "Oh, I believe it." Playing leapfrog from roof to roof, I knew they may not like my methods, but the results couldn't be argued. We never would have made it this far if we had to fight through the streets. Leaping onto the government center would be tricky because soldiers were positioned at the top. We had to take them out at the last two buildings, but there had only been three or four on each. "Michael, I think two of us need to go ahead. We'll be able to get there without being noticed. The rest should line the roof and pick off as many as they can. They'll be drawn over here, it will give the troops below a chance to advance, and we'll be able to get behind them while they're separated and pick off any that you don't."

Moving to stand next to me, he said, "Agreed. I'm going with Misty, the rest of you take cover and as soon as we're in position, start firing." Shaking his head, he took off running, and we hit the edge at the same time, flying through the air. I cleared the lip of the next roof, but unfortunately he didn't. Slamming into the side, he was able to catch it with his hands and racing back, I gripped his pack and helped him pull himself over. "I don't care what I have to do or who I have to kill, I'm never doing that again," he shuddered pulling himself up.

"Then I guess you won't be coming into the caverns," I said, moving for cover.

"You're not going to tell me that there aren't floors in the caverns, now are you?" he snapped, as our boys started to pick off the soldiers.

"Oh, there's floors, but do you think that the fighting there is going to be any different than this?" I said with a smirk, before going silent as two soldiers moved our way to take position.

Taking my knife from its cover on my leg, we waited until they were in position. As one we moved, wrapping a hand around their mouths and putting the blade through their backs into their lungs. Dropping them where the others would see, we moved and waited for the next set to take their place. After the third time, I signaled for Michael to stop. There were still a dozen soldiers up here, but if we took many more out like this, they'd call for reinforcements. They're all lined up in the front of the building, only splitting off to move over to this section that was no longer protected by the soldiers of the building we now occupied. We'd have to take out the soldiers on the building on the other side of the government center or we'd be caught in their crosshairs. We slowly moved back as two soldiers came to take the place of the ones we just disposed of. Using the equipment as cover, we made our way around to get in position on the other side. Three soldiers could be seen moving there. I'm sure there were more, but for now we just needed to take them out. Pulling his rifle off his back, Michael set it up as I kept watch. I wasn't worried about being heard, we'd just blend in with the rest of the noise—it was being seen that would get us killed.

He was good; I'd give him that. Three soldiers, three shots in under a minute and he solved the problem. Falling back, I pulled off my own rifle—it was now or never. Only seven soldiers remained, the others having picked more off. Separating, we opened fire, and they didn't know what hit them. Clearing the roof, we signaled to the others keeping watch as they made their jumps. Now that we controlled the roof, the troops on the ground that had been pinned down were advancing against the soldiers on the ground. Making for the door, we weren't quick enough—a soldier that we didn't see from the neighboring building opened fire, killing two of our men before we were able to take him down. Unable to do anything for them, we kept going. The stairwell was empty. Keeping quiet, we went toward the dim sound of gunfire. Stopping at the corner before a main hall, we heard soldiers. No, not soldiers—the communications room. Seeing a glint out of the corner of my eye, I turned and smiled, inching my way toward it. Shaking off the hand that tried to restrain me, I pointed toward the mirror on the wall. Snatching it up, I scooted back, passing it up to Michael. Using it to see around the corner before snatching back, he held up two fingers. There were two soldiers in the hall. Signaling for us to stay, he motioned for Justin to follow. Tensely, we waited until Justin came back, signaling for us to go. Moving to Michael, who stood next to the door, he motioned for silence, listening to the voices coming from the room.

"Your soldiers have lost Twin Rivers and the outlying towns and villages. My people overran them with pitchforks and stones. I backed your government because President Vellion gave assurances that it would be a quick victory," a man screamed in a high-pitched voice. "I was to be the new President!"

"Shut that fool up," a second voice growled.

"Commander, the line has fallen, rebel troops are rushing the government building. We're trapped, sir."

"Can we hold the building long enough for reinforcements to arrive?" the commander asked.

"No, sir, no reinforcements will be sent, there are none." The sound of approaching forces could be heard as gunfire grew closer.

"What do you mean there are no reinforcements?" the man with the high-pitched voice screamed.

"Shut up, Kingman," the commander snapped the sound of something hitting the floor echoed. From the hardened looks on the men's faces around me at the name, I knew they knew who it was.

"I'll not be told to shut up by the likes of you, do you have any idea who I am?" Kingman shrilly said.

"Yes, I know exactly who you are. A stupid fool who actually thought we were going to make a slave president." He laughed harshly at the sputtering man. "Since we're going to die, Kingman, I think it's time you got a quick lesson in the truth. We used you. Just like we use all slaves as tools. Each one of you fools who betrayed your people thought that you were going to receive a place among our society and you were—as slaves. The only thing that I'll truly regret is not getting a go at that daughter of yours. If she was anything like your wife, she would have been a wonderful addition to the brothels. Now, since your use is over, I'm going to take great pleasure at finally killing you."

"You, you can't kill me. President Vellion assured me that I was in charge that…" Hitting Michael's arm I mouthed "we need him alive," and, nodding his head, though I could tell he'd like nothing better than to let the bastard die, he motioned to the others. Moving in, we opened fire with all eyes on the sniveling coward who was hiding behind a desk. It was short and sweet. Unprepared, we were able to take most of them prisoner and with Kingman's distraction they were unable to dispose of anything. The room was more filled than we thought; there were several high-raking government officials that thought they could bluff their way out. Securing the prisoners and the room, we left a pair of guards and moved out.

The last of the soldiers were being chased right toward us. Opening fire, they were caught between us and the troops coming up behind them. Seeing that they were trapped, they tried to surrender, but I was having none of that and kept firing until the last fell to the floor, ignoring the yells to stop.

"They were surrendering," Michael yelled into my face, hitting my gun from my hand. Turning my back to him, I went to walk back the way we had just came, wanting to visit the prisoners. "I'm talking to you, Misty"–

—when I kept moving, a hand gripped me and pulled me around—"is this who you want to be?" he growled, gripping my face to force me to look at the soldiers who I had just killed. "Do you want to be like them? Because if you keep this up, you're no better than them."

I don't know what he expected his words to do. With a slow hand, I reached up and gently gripped the hand at my chin, removing it so I could look at him. "Since they're dead, we'll never know if they meant to surrender," I replied softly, dropping his hand. "And since I'm alive and we have appeared to have won, I think I am better than them. Now you have work to do and so do I," I finished, walking away. The sound of cheering echoed outside in the streets. They won and they were rejoicing in their freedom. To me though, it was just the beginning. Nothing had changed for me; I was still just as broken and alone. I was still surrounded by the darkness and living in it. I knew what he wanted me to see, that by my actions I was no better than they were. I don't know how he still denied the truth after seeing the things that I had done. I don't know how he didn't realize that I was just like them. I was what they had made me—a soulless killer. Instead of hiding from what I was, I embraced it. I had more questions than ever and moving forward, I didn't look back, knowing what I had to do to answer them.

Chapter 24

Two weeks had passed since their victory. They were still celebrating though they mourned those that had been lost. The government officials involved with the Loyalist city's attempted coup were being held for trial. The council led by Victor had seized control, taking their place. The City to the West had been quiet, making no attempt to try again so far, though emissaries had been sent to speak of peace, saying that a rogue fraction had been behind this and not the official government. Victor and the council had been meeting with them behind closed doors.

Moving through the Stone City, I watched as its occupants still cleaned the streets of debris as other teams worked on rebuilding what had been destroyed. Though all of the towns and villages had suffered in some form of attack, most of the fight had been centralized in this area, making Twin Rivers and the Stone City the hardest hit in destruction and deaths. People nodded to me as I passed, though they don't meet my eye. What I had done to the prisoners made it into the general population. Not just what I had done to the men at the barracks and in the hall, but what I had done to those we had taken in that room. I wish that I could say that the thought of the way I had tortured them for information made me sick, but it didn't. Michael had gone and seized control of the troops, giving orders to secure the Stone City while contacting the council and other rebel commanders to see where help was still needed and to share information. By the time he returned to check on the prisoners, more than a day had passed, though he had arranged for guards to rotate the duty of guarding them.

What was left by the time he came was not pretty. Those I hadn't gotten to yet were sniveling messes. Forced to watch my methods on the Loyalist commander and his soldiers, the politicians begged to volunteer information. The bloody mass attached to the chair was what was left of the commander. It had taken hours to break him, but once I did, the information that he gave me was worth it. Sitting across from him, covered in blood with my knife firmly in my hand, was how Michael found me. He yelled at the guards who were outside instead of in the room, as they hurriedly explained that they were following my orders. Walking in, he took the scene in with a sweep of his eyes before landing on me. I could feel his gaze boring into my back, but I just sat there watching the creature before me that moaned for death. The retching sounds of the guards joined those of the other captives, who upon seeing Michael enter begged to be spared. Pleading to tell him anything that he wished to know if he would just help them get away from me.

Slowly, I rose from the chair, causing the whole room to tense. Turning, I saw that the guards were gripping the hilts of their guns as they looked at me in horror. Sliding the knife back into the holster at my leg, I walked forward. Hurriedly, they moved to the side except Michael, who just looked at me with an unreadable expression. Walking out the door, I saw that a crowd had gathered. Stumbling upon themselves, they moved back just as swiftly as the guards in the room upon seeing me, most adverting their gaze. I never said a word nor was one said to me by those I passed. They all but raced to get out of my way. Keeping my pace, no more than a leisurely stroll, I walked from the Stone City and through Twin Rivers. I don't know how long I walked or how long it took before I came to the river that the town was named for. The river where we first met these people that had caused my life to change again. Just like every other change in my life, it wasn't for the better. I didn't stop walking when I reached the river; I just walked in fully clothed. The water around me turned instantly red. Dunking my head under, I systematically washed away my sins, making them invisible for others to see. That's all that mattered, was what others could see. They were all the same. As long as the outside was beautiful, it didn't matter how dark and evil what it hid was.

The water ran clear by the time a group of troops was sent to get me. Opening my eyes, I turned slowly to face them. They stood back from me as if they were afraid to approach. Staring at them, I watched as one turned and motioned to someone. A girl moved forward. It took a moment for me to place her. "Why are you here?" I asked the nervous girl as she walked past the troops to the edge of the water. When she just stood there frozen, I moved toward her, stopping when she hurriedly stepped back. Not having the patience for this, I continued on stepping out from the water, but going no closer as the troops gripped their guns. "Why are you here?" I asked again. When all I got was silence I lost my patience. "If you're here to kill me, get on with it."

"We're not here to hurt you," the girl blurted out, finally raising her gaze to mine. "I don't know if you remember me, but my name is Keely."

Interrupting her, I said, "I know who you are, now answer me. Why are you here?"

"They thought," she stuttered, before taking a breath and continuing, "they thought that you'd feel more comfortable if someone you know came to get you and escorted you to a living unit so you could rest."

Closing my eyes, trying to hold on to my patience, I opened them and smiled grimly at the poor lamb in front of me. "Will I be allowed to leave this living unit after I've rested?" I asked.

"Yes," she said, looking at me confusedly, "why wouldn't you?"

Oh, I don't know, the fact that an armed trigger-happy troop had been sent to fetch me might be some indication, but instead I just shook my head and walked forward. I don't know who jumped farther, the girl Keely or my armed escort as they moved to give me a wide path. Rolling my eyes, I walked past and made my way back. They didn't have to worry about me escaping—the answers I needed where still there and I wouldn't be leaving without them. After a while the girl Keely moved up to walk next to me, still keeping a distance between us, but showing more courage than the group of men that surrounded me.

"They say you're the reason that we won," she said, finally breaking the silence.

"They say that, do they? And how was I the reason your people won?" I asked, amused.

"The troops said that you got the communications block jammed and freed the barracks troops to fight. It's the reason we were able to hold Twin Rivers and warn the Stone City," she babbled, stopping at the look I threw her.

Stopping dead, I reached over, grabbing the girl's arm and pulling her to me. Ignoring the troops who pulled their guns, I said, "Your people won the battle, Keely. When the lines fell, they left behind the safety of their shelters and fought with their bare hands. No one person did anything; when people think like that, they give a single person too much power and that is dangerous," I spat, letting her go and continuing on. I would have to move quickly and get my answers or I wasn't going to live long enough to have a chance.

The rest of the walk was silent and I was surprised when I was brought to the original place that Tristian and I first stayed. Going in, I wasn't followed. The door was closed behind me, but it wasn't locked from the outside. I suppose they were trying to maintain an illusion that I wasn't a prisoner. I guess that if these people thought of me as a hero they would have a hard time explaining why I was imprisoned. Going to the bathroom, I quickly showered, leaving my damp clothes on the ground, only stopping long enough to take my knife. Taking a flowing dress from the closet, I pulled it on, putting my knife in the deep pocket that was slit into it. I looked just as harmless as I had the first day I arrived here. Going to the bed, I crawled in. I don't know how long it had been since I slept, but I felt the exhaustion and I fought it. I fought it because I knew that it would bring the dreams. Eventually it didn't matter and it took me. It took me right back into the darkness that never left me. The darkness that always lived within and grew with each dark deed I was forced to commit to stay in the light.

My thoughts were interrupted as one of my constant escorts stepped up into my path. "Council leader Victor wishes to see you now," he said, before quickly stepping back. Not bothering to acknowledge his words, I turned and walked to the government's center. The coward was finally going to see me. For two weeks every excuse had been sent as to why he was unavailable and I guess he had finally run out. Stepping up the steps, I ignored it as everyone turned to look and whisper. What they whispered could be anything—to some I was a hero and to others a danger that should be put down. More troops joined my escort as I was directed to a door down a long hall. The troops who guarded it waited until I was almost upon them before opening it.

Walking into the large office, I went to the seat before the table that Victor and the council sat at, not acknowledging the others littered around it. I guess this was not to be a private meeting. Sitting down, I looked straight at Victor, careful to hold back my smile and keep my face blank when he couldn't hold my eyes and waited. The seconds ticked by and the other occupants began it fidget, nervous at the battle of wills.

Finally, unable to take it, Victor broke and spoke first. "Misty, I'm sorry that I wasn't able to see you before this, but with what's been going on we've been trying to give our people some sense of stability in its government."

Tilting my head to the side, I kept my eyes glued to Victor's and let a small smile grace my lips. "Yes, I've heard that you've been meeting with the Loyalist city's representatives to discuss a peace treaty." Everyone at the table suddenly found something more interesting than me to look at.

Keeping his sympathetic grandfather look, Victor nodded his head. "Yes, we've been meeting with the city's representatives. It would seem that a rogue fraction of their government was responsible for the attempted takeover and they were hoping to avoid any more bloodshed."

"And I'm sure now that your council has seized control of the government that you also wish to avoid any further bloodshed," I said, instead of calling him the liar that he was.

It was harder for him to hold the look this time. "We have taken heavy casualties..." he began.

"They would have been much heavier if I hadn't interceded," I interrupted. "In fact, if it hadn't been for Tristian and I, you would have had no clue that your whole government hadn't already sold you to them and were just waiting for a chance to hand you over," I told them pleasantly. If the bastards thought I was going to make it easy on them, they could think again.

There it was, now the real Victor was going to come out and play. "While we are grateful to what you have done, Misty, and acknowledge the sacrifices that you have made, you can't expect us in good conscience to risk our battle-weary people against a fortified city," he responded, unable to keep the anger from his voice.

"Expect a government to keep their word, Victor? Now why would I do that?" I taunted.

"You little ingrate. We gave you protection when no one else would have. How many of my people died to make sure that you lived?" he hissed, spittle coming out from his lips.

I couldn't help but laugh. "Died for me, Victor, are you kidding? You know, I fell for it all, you were good." Shaking my head, I wiped a tear from my eye. "It was the commander at the barracks that helped me put it all together. Tell me, Victor, how long were you playing both sides? I mean it must have been quite a surprise when they couldn't find me and went on a killing spree to prove a point." Looking at his daughter Karen, who was behind him, I said, "And you, dragging your dead daughter and using her as a prop. That speech, you knew exactly what your father was up to, so you made sure he wouldn't be suspected of being the traitor," I said, shaking my head at the fear my words brought to her eyes before she masked it with hate. Like a cornered rat, his eyes darted before he covered them with indignation ready to brazen his way out. Holding my hand to stop his words, I said, "Not that I'm not sure that the story you will tell these fools after I leave will not have them believing your every word, but I don't want to hear it." Standing up, I moved to the door, and stopping before reaching it, I turned and gazed around the whole room, nodding my head to Michael and Johnathon before turning back to the council. "I knew that you were not going to help my people, yet I still helped yours. I did it because it was the right thing to do. You all look at me like I'm going to attack you at any moment, like I'm a monster." Allowing a grim smile to grace my lips, I said, "I'm a killer and I make no excuses nor apologies for it. The things that they whisper I've done—I don't deny them. I'm a product of the world around me. The difference between me and every other person in this room is that I accept it. You stand here in judgement of me and yet I can honestly say I am better than each of you. I've kept my word while you have proved you are no different than those you fought to be free from." Bowing my head, I opened the door, startling the guards on the other side and walked away without looking back.

Chapter 25

It's time. Victor is not going to take what I've done lying down, but the funny thing is, it's the daughter I'm more concerned about. I shouldn't have done that, but I had to know the truth. Changing my clothing, my mind went to the journey I was about to make and I wondered again if it is not just a form of suicide. I had a way into the Loyalist city and the caverns that, if the commander who I tortured is correct, I will never be discovered, using and old system of drainage pipes. He had used them often, abducting women from the caverns, and to get out of the city so he could have privacy with them. Stepping over my unconscious guards, I grabbed my packs. Keely had been a great help gathering the things I needed. The girl had been my companion over the last two weeks and I hoped that she wouldn't suffer from helping me.

Closing the door behind me, I went to the stairs, using them to get to the ground floor. Waiting until it was clear, I used the same route Johnathon once took us on and went out through the back of the building. Keeping my hood up, I blended with the crowd, making my way through the streets and into the woods. My guards wouldn't be discovered for a few hours when their relief came.

Victor would be too busy digging himself from the hole I just dug him to send an assassin for a while yet. Avoiding the scouts in the woods was rather easy. I already knew where they were. It was just the one at the bridge that would have to be dealt with. When I could see the bridge, I stopped. What stood in front of it I should have expected. Fingering my knife, I gazed at the two men blocking the bridge as my mind made a decision I hoped I didn't regret. Leaving it sheathed, I approached them, going to the center of the path so they would see me.

"Did you even go to look for me at my housing unit or did you come straight here?" I asked, as I approached them holding my hands from my body so they could see I was unarmed.

"I wanted to go, but Michael said you wouldn't be there and talked me into coming here," Johnathon answered with a small smile.

Stopping about twenty feet from them, I asked, "So why are you here blocking my path instead of at your council meeting?"

"Beautiful day for a walk," Michael replied, looking up at the sky before turning back to me. "Are your guards dead?"

"No, they're a little tied up and weren't able to join me on my walk." I sighed.

"What you said about Victor—" he started.

"Was all true," I finished.

Nodding his head, he said, "Victor quickly took control of the meeting after you left. Saying that the shocks that you've suffered in your life have caused you to unhinge. That you were lashing out because we were creating a treaty of peace between the Loyalist city and us. He stated that you just didn't understand. That though we would eventually help those in the caverns, if they were even there and it wasn't part of your delusion, it would be through a process of negotiation. Then he dismissed us all saying that he needed to rest."

Yeah, I bet he did.

"So you decided to come see me and make sure that I wasn't going on a murdering rampage in my unhinged state?" I smirked.

Instead of smiling, he looked me dead in the eye. "No, we came to make sure you weren't murdered to keep you quiet."

"Well that explains you two, but what about the rest of your people surrounding us? What are they here for?"

Signaling with his hand, I watched as what was left of the unit that I served next to just weeks before came out of the woods. "They are here because they feel like going for a walk, too."

Looking at all of them, I said, "The safest walk for you to take is behind you, the way you came. I'm going to be hunted from both sides and anyone caught with me will not be treated kindly." When they all just smiled at me, I couldn't help the answering one that graced my lips as I tried again. "You'll be deserters. Victor will have you branded as traitors."

"I think that is an understatement and I think we're wasting time. Johnathon will be heading back to be our eyes inside, doing what he can to run interference when needed. The rest of us are with you," Michael said, before pointing to another man who hadn't joined us, but stayed in his post up in the tree. "That is Daryl, one of the troops that you released from the barracks, as far as he is concerned, no one came this way. So I think that covers everything except this"—he pulled out a folded-up paper from his jacket that he held out to me—"your map of the caverns, I picked it up when Victor wasn't looking, figuring that we needed it a little more." I had given it to Victor thinking that I was going to die in the attack.

Stepping forward and closing the distance between us, I took the map from his hand. Looking down at it, I gave them one last chance to walk away. "Tristian is alive and being held in the city. They haven't killed him yet, as far as I know, because he won't give them the information on how we escaped. He still lives because they couldn't catch me. The city commander that I questioned gave me information on how to enter the city and the caverns without being seen." Looking up into Michael's eyes, I said, "I'm going in to get him if he still lives. Than I'm going into the caverns."

"Well, I guess we had better get going," he said, the look in his eyes unreadable, but firm.

"Alright, than I guess we have our orders. Misty, darling, it's been a pleasure," Johnathon said, breaking the moment. Stepping up to me, he lifted me up in a hug and swung me around before sealing his lips to mine in a quick kiss. Stepping back, he slapped Michael's back and headed down the path back to town.

Bemused, I watched him go before turning back, rolling my eyes at the scowl on Michael's face. I moved past him and headed across the bridge. If the sound of footsteps didn't tell me they were there, Justin's staged whisper comment would have. "I think I'm back to not liking her. Here we are, my first real vacation and where does she take me. Some place new? Oh, no not her. With her it's the same old thing, running for our lives and getting shot at. Well, she better not be expecting me to go flying through the air again. I'm telling you all right now, I will not be jumping from any roofs…"

I couldn't help but smile at the good-natured ribbing going on between them. Here they were, going with me to an almost certain death and they were joking about it. As Michael moved next to me, I let out a breath that I hadn't realized I had been holding. I wasn't alone. No matter what was to come, I wasn't alone and I didn't know why that brought me comfort when it should have filled me with dread. Like Tristian and my sisters, they were now my responsibility to care for and like Tristian and my sisters, I wouldn't be able to protect them. But as we left the bridge and the forest began to surround us, the only thing I could think of was that in the darkness I wouldn't be alone…

www.ingramcontent.com/pod-product-compliance
Lightning Source LLC
Chambersburg PA
CBHW061324170626
46817CB00001B/305